PENGUIN METRO READS
OUR STORY NEEDS NO FILTER

Sudeep Nagarkar has authored eight bestselling novels—*Few Things Left Unsaid, That's the Way We Met, It Started with a Friend Request, Sorry, You're Not My Type, You're the Password to My Life, You're Trending in My Dreams, She Swiped Right into My Heart* and *All Rights Reserved for You*—and is the recipient of the Youth Achievers Award. He has been featured on the *Forbes India* longlist of the most influential celebrities for three consecutive years. He has given guest lectures in renowned institutes such as IITs and organizations like TEDx. His books have been translated into various languages, including Hindi, Marathi and Telugu.

Connect with Sudeep via his:
Facebook fan page: /sudeepnagarkar
Facebook profile: /nagarkarsudeep
Twitter: sudeep_nagarkar
Instagram: sudeepnagarkar
Snapchat: nagarkarsudeep
Website: www.sudeepnagarkar.in

D1577764

BY THE SAME AUTHOR

All Rights Reserved for You
She Swiped Right into My Heart
You're Trending in My Dreams
You're the Password to My Life
Sorry, You're Not My Type
It Started with a Friend Request
That's the Way We Met
Few Things Left Unsaid

SUDEEP NAGARKAR

our
story
needs
no filter

Penguin
metro reads

An imprint of Penguin Random House

PENGUIN METRO READS

USA | Canada | UK | Ireland | Australia
New Zealand | India | South Africa | China

Penguin Metro Reads is part of the Penguin Random House group of companies
whose addresses can be found at global.penguinrandomhouse.com

Published by Penguin Random House India Pvt. Ltd
7th Floor, Infinity Tower C, DLF Cyber City,
Gurgaon 122 002, Haryana, India

Penguin
Random House
India

First published in Penguin Metro Reads by Penguin Random House India 2017

Copyright © Sudeep Nagarkar 2017

All rights reserved

10 9 8 7 6 5 4 3 2 1

This is a work of fiction. Names, characters, places and incidents are either the
product of the author's imagination or are used fictitiously and any resemblance
to any actual person, living or dead, events or locales is entirely coincidental.

ISBN 9788184007442

Typeset in Adobe Garamond Pro by Manipal Digital Systems, Manipal
Printed at Thomson Press India Ltd, New Delhi

This book is sold subject to the condition that it shall not, by way of trade
or otherwise, be lent, resold, hired out, or otherwise circulated without the
publisher's prior consent in any form of binding or cover other than that in
which it is published and without a similar condition including this condition
being imposed on the subsequent purchaser.

www.penguin.co.in

Prologue

Dear friend,

These days I have come to question the aim of religion. It feels like a fruitless pursuit, wherein we turn away from logic and reason. We constantly look outward for inspiration, when interestingly enough the answers lie within. I have been a witness to the adverse effect religion seems to have on human welfare and this is why I have come to question its presence in our lives. It's merely an illusion where we blindly follow the ideologies our communities have laid down for us.

He called it Kraanti—a fight for our existence and a fight for acceptance. This, I feel, is a misinterpretation that will not only lead vulnerable minds like mine astray, but will also lead to destruction. What is even more worrying is that he is a puppet himself, dancing to the tunes of those who are powerful.

The movement revealed the hypocrisy of those in power. They only saw one thing when they looked at a student—a vote. I joined MGU with the hope of learning and meeting new people and initially I did make a few friends, but my loved ones were pushed away as I surrendered to the wrong ideologies. I know you had high hopes for me, but despite that I lost your faith and your friendship. All I can say is that I was caught up in the moment. They say love makes you strong but he knew it was also my weakness, and he used it against me. Until reality hit, I did not even realize that the words I spoke to the crowd were not my own. I uttered them not out of conviction, but of fear of repercussion.

But this explanation may be unnecessary. When you need to explain yourself to the ones you love, I think it's time to move on. But somewhere, something holds me to you all. I remember you warning me, 'They are storytellers. The words they spin will change you, change your outlook,' but I never paid heed to it. Maybe I was wrong all this time, to think I understood the emotions of life. Looking back, I now see myself falling into a void. I feel pathetic.

Your friend, forever.

One

30 April 2016

'The Hindu society must be one of the most brutal societies in the world,' a professor said to her students. 'It is deep-rooted in violence.'

'Isn't Hinduism all about peace?' a student challenged. 'To suppress the devil inside and become righteous? It was never about violence. You, as a professor of MGU, should pass on the correct information rather than fabricating stories.'

It was at that moment when Krishna, the leader of the All India Student Council (AISC), one of the student political parties of the Mahatma Gandhi University (MGU), Delhi, overheard the discussion while passing by. Hearing the student intervene, he entered the classroom.

Krishna was simply dressed: a casual shirt, jeans and chappals. The debate was happening after regular working hours in the college—nothing out of the ordinary for the students of the AISC.

'Salaam, everyone,' Krishna greeted everyone. Then turning to the student, he said, 'We are not against any religion but those Hindu organizations that force their views on innocent minorities and the lower castes are not to be tolerated. I am from a backward family and I know what it feels like to be one. They want Hindu Raj to prevail in India by barring the reserved castes from entering politics. If the minorities pick up weapons they are called Naxalites, but if someone else does it, it becomes nationalism.'

The student who had raised the objection fell silent.

Krishna went on. 'Today, nationalism is nothing but bad-mouthing our neighbours. Only Brahmins are allowed to speak freely; Dr Ambedkar is remembered only as a Dalit and not as a scholar. We don't need a certificate of patriotism from the Akhil Bhartiya Chatra Parishad. These fascist forces want everyone to blindly follow their ideologies and do not entertain differing opinions. They are denying our right to speak out against caste discrimination.'

Encouraged by a wave of applause, Krishna continued, 'Despite this wave of intolerance, we have to have full faith in the Constitution of India. If someone tries to challenge it, we will retaliate. We must debate the concept of violence with them. The caste system is one of the biggest problems in this country, and this culture of exploitation, along with that of Brahminism, should be destroyed. We must educate people about the caste system and bring reservation into every sector including the private. We stand for equal rights. We stand for the right to live.'

Taken over by a wave of passion, Krishna concluded the session along with the professor. Once everyone had left, he went up to the student who had objected to the criticism of Hinduism. The student had come to the session on Krishna's advice. He had been the victim of discrimination merely hours ago, and Krishna had informed him of an organization that worked to preserve the right of the lower castes. The student was still a little hesitant and Krishna knew he had to proceed cautiously.

'See, our organization is for the youth of our community. Youth like you who have suffered. The motive of our movement is to spread the correct virtues of humanity and to help people educate themselves about basic human rights. We have a core section in the AISC wherein the more dedicated students are given important tasks to execute. Teachers come from different universities to guide us in the right direction. Would you like to join that team and spread our cause?'

The student nodded, slightly confused but totally hypnotized by Krishna's words. Krishna took that as a yes and welcomed him into their group with a handshake. The overwhelmed student, mollified by the handshake, still felt that there was something about Krishna which he couldn't quite figure out.

'I want to give you a task. I have full faith in you and your courage. On the completion of this task, there is scope for promotion. More recognition, more responsibilities,' Krishna said.

'What's it all about?' asked the student.

'You have to deliver some parcels to Ambala. It's a bit far, but don't worry, everything will be taken care of. Ever been to Ambala?'

'Never.'

'Our organization offers help to those who do not have access to basic rights like education through these parcels. We have mediators to make sure these parcels reach them safely.'

'These parcels . . . ?'

'They contain books and other stationery. You need to deliver them to Ambala. Once you do it, you will have made your first contribution towards our movement, Kraanti.'

Sensing his apprehension, Krishna encouraged his new compatriot, 'I trust you. It's not a big deal and you can do it. You don't want the students of your community to suffer, right?'

'When do I have to leave?'
'Tomorrow.'

The next morning, the student was briefed about his task. A car awaited him along with his personal escort and he was given five thousand rupees for his expenses.

Throughout the journey, his past flashed before him. It had been tough but Krishna had eventually made him realize his purpose. He didn't want others to be tormented just because they were Dalits or were deemed unworthy by the Indian religious elite. Krishna and his movement, Kraanti, claimed to fight for their rights. It was his job to execute the first step towards their betterment.

On his arrival, there was someone to receive him and to verify his identity. He was taken to a room in an old building and was told to wait for further instructions. The locality looked old and congested, but despite his creeping suspicions, he waited calmly within the cracked walls of the room.

Suddenly, there was a knock at the door. He went to open it, but by the time he reached, the passageway stood empty. He spotted an envelope lying on the floor. There was a message inside—a delivery address and a time. Strange, he thought. Why couldn't someone tell him this in person? Pushing aside his doubts, he decided to carry on with his mission. He trusted Krishna. Getting into the car, he looked at the address again. There was not much time left, so he quickly fed the given location into Google Maps and asked the driver to follow his directions. As the car crawled into narrow lanes, he became a little nervous, until the hoarding mentioned in the envelope showed up. It was similar to the old building he had been put in. Walking up to the door, he knocked carefully.

'Just leave it outside. I am a little busy and can't open the door right now,' said a voice from inside.

Conflicted, he asked, 'Are you sure?'

'Yes. Krishna told me about you.'

For a moment there was absolute silence. He tried calling Krishna but could not get through to his number. He hesitated for a moment before leaving the heavy boxes outside the door and departing.

On the way back, he received a message from Krishna.

'Good job. My man said he received the boxes in perfect condition. You are now officially a part of Kraanti.'

Two

23 December 2015

'What are you reading? You seem completely absorbed,' Jai said as he sat down beside Raghu. 'Have you realized you missed your class? The psychology lecture is over.'

'It's a book by John Grisham—very interesting, especially the protagonist who is such a complex character. One minute you like him, and the other minute you hate him! And he's so vulnerable. He'll believe anything he's told,' Raghu replied, turning a page, still engrossed.

'I get it. Basically he's you.' Jai laughed.

Raghu looked up. He was not amused. 'I mean . . .' Jai attempted an explanation. 'Don't you behave in a similar way? Your emotions allow people to convince you about anything in minutes. Isn't that a bad thing?'

'Of course it isn't.'

The boys were interrupted by Megha, the third person in their friend circle.

'Hey! Reading Grisham? Have you reached the part where—' Megha had a knack for giving out spoilers, which irked Raghu to no end.

'Don't say another word!' Raghu cut her short, putting a finger to his lips.

'Fine, I'm not saying another word. But I just love his character descriptions and how well drawn out even the minor characters are; they stay with you long after the book is over! I can't even write a Facebook post without breaking into a sweat,' she joked.

'And yet you keep writing those long posts,' Jai teased her.

'I love posting my views, no matter what the topic.'

'Politics is waiting for people like you.'

'No way,' said Megha, shaking her head.

Raghu, still stuck in the previous discussion, said, 'See . . . now do you get it? Grisham makes you feel for the characters; even Megha agrees.'

'I got it the moment you described him. All I'm saying is some day, someone will convince you of something, just like they did the main character. Ask Megha, she'll tell you I'm right.'

'Who? Raghu? Anyone can take him for a ride!'

The three close friends continued their animated discussion, sitting inside the campus café. It was a popular hang-out among the students, located right next to the entry gates. A couple of dogs were barking furiously outside.

'Did you hear our prime minister's speech yesterday?' asked Megha.

'Yeah,' the boys replied in chorus. Both knew what was coming next.

'I loved the colour of his Nehru jacket. How does he carry such vibrant colours so well at his age?'

'Mitrooooon,' Raghu said in a mocking tone.

'No jokes about him please,' Jai protested.

'Are you a bhakt?'

'If respecting our prime minister makes me a bhakt, then I guess I am,' Jai said, sounding a little annoyed.

'You guys are impossible. Always ready to get into a debate,' interjected Megha.

'That's how we express our friendship.' Jai smiled.

'Argh, these dogs barking collectively is getting on my nerves,' Raghu said, shifting his eyes from Jai to the dogs. They were sitting close to the café's exit and had a good view of the street.

Raghu noticed a man buying a packet of biscuits to feed the dogs. Nearby, there was a small girl, around eight or nine years of age, carrying a baby on one arm while trying to collect scraps of discarded food with her other hand. Clearly hungry, she picked up bits of bread, tomatoes and half-eaten burgers from the roadside. Raghu felt a war of emotions raging within: respect for the man feeding the stray dogs, at the same time a rising anger at his nonchalant attitude towards the young girl who evidently had little to eat. How could people not know how best to use their money? The more he looked, the angrier he got. Looking for a vent for his emotions, he looked around for a stone to throw at the dogs. Raghu disliked animals, especially dogs, but the inequality pricked him more.

The moment he threw the stone, he felt a pat on his shoulder. He turned around to see Ruhi looking at him fiercely. 'You are so cruel; just because animals cannot speak, it doesn't mean you can torment them in such a way. That's wrong.'

'Look at that hungry girl. She quietly starves while the man next to her spends his money to feed stray dogs. That's wrong too.'

'You said you loved animals, especially dogs.' Raghu had lied to her about his dislike for dogs since he knew she loved them.

'I know, Ruhi, but I love humans more.'

'Whatever. You are sick. If you care so much about that girl, why don't you go and feed her instead of just blaming others? Don't complain about the actions of others if you do nothing yourself,' Ruhi shot back and turned to leave.

A few days ago

'If your dog's tail is wagging, is it just he who is happy to see me or are you both?' Raghu asked as he walked over to Ruhi, who was playing with a cute puppy.

'He's not a dog. He is my baby.' She smiled, taking the dog in her lap.

Raghu seemed unconvinced, but carried on casually, 'Yes, of course.'

Ruhi had only recently started spending time with their group. She was close to Megha but didn't know the others too well. Raghu, who had taken a liking to her, didn't want to risk anything that might ruin his chances of getting close to her.

So he lied. 'They are so captivating. They can lift my mood in a second,' he said smoothly.

'Same here, puppies are the best way to relieve your stress.' Ruhi looked up and smiled at Raghu.

'Do you watch movies?' Raghu asked abruptly. Sensing Ruhi's confusion, he went on, 'I am sure you have seen all those movies where things are escalating between the good guy and the bad guy and then the good guy's dog starts barking because he senses that his owner is in some sort of trouble. And then suddenly he breaks free and saves him.'

Seeing her scepticism, Raghu continued to ramble, 'No, really, I even hate the people who are cruel to animals.'

He tried to prove his affection by stroking the puppy's head.

'You know, last year we marched the streets to protest against harassment of street dogs. If I had known you then, I would have invited you along,' Ruhi said.

'We . . . ?'

'I am a part of PETA—People for the Ethical Treatment of Animals,' Ruhi responded with pride.

'Oh, I see. I assume then that you are a vegetarian as well.' Raghu felt a burp bubbling up. The butter chicken that he had had for lunch was not sitting well in his stomach.

'I am a Brahmin, but even if I wasn't, I wouldn't have enjoyed eating animals.'

Raghu let out a small burp.

'Do something! Stop her,' Raghu pleaded desperately to Megha.

'Ruhi . . . wait!' Megha screamed, running after her.

If anyone could appease Ruhi, it was Megha. She knew that Raghu liked Ruhi, and while she was aware that they had nothing in common, his efforts spurred her into action.

'You are taking it the wrong way. It was not Raghu's fault . . .' Megha tried to pacify her.

'I saw it myself. Don't try to defend him.'

'It was I who provoked him. I know you love dogs, I told him to do it to get your attention. I am sorry.' Megha's performance seemed to mollify Ruhi.

Though not totally convinced, Ruhi trusted Megha after having spent so much time with her. Jai also pitched in. The three friends—Raghu, Jai and Megha—had an emotional connect difficult to put into words. They always stood up for one another. As everyone headed towards the canteen, Raghu caught up with Ruhi and apologized.

'Sorry for the—'

'It's okay,' Ruhi cut him short with a smile.

A wave of relief washed over him. Not just that—her smile unleashed a multitude of emotions in Raghu. It was as if a cloud of innocent love had descended upon him unexpectedly. He was elated, and despite the heavy crowd in the canteen, he felt serene. The spell was broken only when he heard Jai ask, 'Where is Chris? I tried calling him a couple of times but got no response.'

'Where could he have gone that he can't answer our calls?' Raghu added.

'Don't tell me he has gone for a movie alone again,' said Megha.

'You are probably right,' Raghu contemplated, and then looking towards Ruhi, added, 'You know, he is kind of crazy. Whenever there's a new SRK movie, he insists on watching it alone.'

'And that too a matinee show! He buys multiple tickets to try and convince people that he is with a group and his friends are just about to arrive. He's not creepy though, just an out-and-out movie buff.'

'Stop bitching about him, he is very sweet. Always stands up for his friends when they need him. Also, there are perks of watching a movie alone; you don't have to share your popcorn with anyone.'

'True. And he never pretends to love something he secretly hates,' Ruhi teased Raghu, as the friends continued bickering playfully. Spending time with friends is the greatest joy. Whether it is sharing a meal together or having a good conversation, there is nothing more fulfilling than being in the company of those you love. Whether or not a college is capable of providing you knowledge to last a lifetime, there is no doubt that it has the ability to provide friendships that will last forever.

As the friends sat at a table, talking among themselves, a group of boys walked towards them menacingly and surrounded them. 'You are Megha, right?' one of the boys asked.

'What's your problem? Please stay away from us, Akhilesh,' Jai said, intervening immediately.

'I am not interested in talking to you. It's better if you stay out of this. This is between me and Megha.'

Jai's hostile stance surprised Megha, as she had seen the two talking to each other around campus.

'Yes, I am Megha,' she replied politely.

'Your Facebook post . . . it's offensive. Delete it or else . . .'

'Or else what?' demanded Jai.

'I told you to stay out of this.'

Turning back to Megha, Akhilesh continued, 'Megha, delete your post because the SCI is against it. Such sensitive issues shouldn't be addressed by mere girls like you.'

Angered by his words, Jai stood up and moved threateningly towards Akhilesh. Megha tried to calm him down—she didn't want any drama. Akhilesh was an aggressive member of the SCI, the Student Council of India, which fought discrimination against students from south India.

'You shouldn't lie about MGU welcoming the culture of the south and our people wholeheartedly. It's not true,' Akhilesh continued his tirade.

'What are you talking about?' Megha was confused. Then Akhilesh flung a printout of her Facebook post on their table.

It read,

This year again during the admission process, we saw people rush to organize caste certificates. Once again the privileged classes in minority communities benefited unduly from caste-based reservation. Those below the poverty line, the lower income groups, are the ones who need help. Income-based reservation will solve our problems as then people from high-income groups will stop getting unnecessary benefits. As I state this, I should also say that our college welcomes students from all parts of India wholeheartedly, be it from the east or the south.

'I don't see anything wrong with it and it's written on my profile. Who the hell asked you to go stalk my profile?' Megha's voice rose; she was finally riled up.

'So you think there is no discrimination? Well then, I have something to confess. I genuinely like you. I'm not saying this to prove my point, but I truly love you and since we are studying in the same university, I don't think you can doubt my abilities to excel in the future. Is my love enough to convince you to marry me sometime in the future?'

Megha was shocked, and Jai and Raghu were furious.

Akhilesh went on, 'You won't, right? Is it because I am from a different caste than yours? Or is it because I'm from the south? Or both? Only when this changes, and caste becomes meaningless, we can talk about the north welcoming the south and its culture.'

'Megha, let's leave. He is just frustrated because he does not have a girlfriend.' Raghu motioned for the group to leave, afraid that Jai would not be able to control his anger much longer.

The episode upset everyone. Hours later, even after Jai and Raghu had regained their composure, Megha was still fuming. The mood only lifted when Chris returned from his movie. Seeing his friends in their dejected state, he demanded to know what had happened. When Raghu narrated the incident, he reacted rather calmly.

'It's okay. Why are you people overthinking the incident? Let him have his opinion, you can have yours. We cannot force someone to change their belief but we can stay away from them. Come on, Ruhi is here today, let's all do something exciting.'

'What can be more exciting than watching a movie alone?' joked Jai.

Chris smiled and turned to Raghu. 'I heard you threw stones at dogs out of sheer desperation. You poor puppy.'

Laughter broke out and the bitter events of the afternoon were soon forgotten. They were once again friends who shared secrets with each other, stood up for each other and laughed together. 'By the way, did you all see the new *Bigg Boss* episode yesterday? Prince expressed his love for Nora. That was so sweet,' Chris said.

'These people will do anything for publicity. Believe me, it's all scripted,' Megha said with a shrug.

'Oh, you are a regular at Salman's house, aren't you? You seem to know what's scripted and what's not,' Jai mocked her.

'Anything that gains popularity is often criticized. There's nothing new about that,' Ruhi said, joining in.

'Aren't films scripted as well? We all enjoy those scenes. There's no need to get into the politics of the show. All I said was that I enjoyed their moments together,' Chris cleared the air.

'But isn't that playing with people's emotions? The director of the show is manipulating it to create controversies where none exist. It's just Indian society, people conjuring drama to line their own pockets,' Megha said, refusing to give in.

'Okay enough, I give up. I hate *Bigg Boss*,' Chris finally said, exasperated.

'Coffee, anyone?' Raghu asked, changing the topic.

'Ask Ruhi. She might need some caffeine to get over you,' said Jai.

Embarrassed, Raghu exclaimed, 'Shut up, you—!'

And just like that, despite their differing opinions, the friends melted into peals of laughter—they had managed to sync their souls through the bond of friendship. The best part was they could always be themselves; no one pretended to be something they were not, yet they always loved being in each other's company. They helped each other in times of trouble and laughed with each other in times of joy. And in the end, isn't that what makes life worth it?

Three

31 December 2015

It was early morning when Jai reached the campus. It was deserted. He was on his bike and in a bad mood. His family had asked him to meet some relatives earlier in the morning who turned out to be very busy, so not only did he waste his time but also his fuel. Still fuming, he was about to enter the gate of his college, when he saw some rowdy youngsters in the distance following a young girl. She had her head down and was walking as fast as she could to remain at a distance from the boys. Jai turned his bike around. As he closed in on the girl, he realized it was Megha. She looked startled and nervous, her fear clearly reflecting on her face.

Megha did not recognize Jai since he had his helmet on, and her nervousness only escalated. First the group of lewd men following her and now an approaching bike—despite her usual bravery in the face of problems, this was too scary a situation. She wanted to scream for help but the only people within hearing distance would have been a couple of construction workers many steps away and a little boy playing football. *They wouldn't come to my rescue*, Megha thought desperately. Even if she were to try and fight them, she would easily be overpowered. *Think, think*, Megha chided herself furiously. Just as she lifted her head to look around for a miraculous appearance of a saviour, Jai stopped his bike next to her.

'Hey, don't worry. Sit behind me.'

This is it, Megha thought. Numb with fear, she stood rooted to the spot. Jai realized that she had not recognized him, but not willing to waste any time, he grabbed her arm and forced her to sit on the bike. The gang dispersed, knowing they had lost their chance. But just as Jai started the engine, Megha screamed, 'Stop right now!'

Jai stopped once they were inside the campus gates and took off his helmet. 'Megha, calm down. You are safe now. What happened? Are you all right?'

'Oh god . . . it's you, Jai.'

The sudden relief from the shooting adrenaline made her go weak in the knees. Jai made her sit on a nearby bench and fetched her some water.

'Is it hurting a lot?' Jai asked, concern lining his voice, as Megha pressed the temple of her head.

'Not really, just . . .'

'Do you get these headaches often?'

'It only happens when I'm under too much stress. Otherwise it's bearable. But there are times when the migraine gets so bad that I cannot move for hours.'

Jai gave her another glass of water. As she slowly regained her composure, embarrassment crept in. She remembered how she had reacted when Jai asked her to get on the bike. He had come to rescue her and she had shouted at him instead. She sipped the water slowly, avoiding his eyes.

'Where are you coming from?' he asked, breaking the silence.

'I had just come out for a morning walk.'

'You shouldn't be doing that in the winter, especially alone.'

Again, an awkward silence.

'Anyway, we should get going. We have the Virgin Tree puja today, remember? The others will be there soon.'

'Oh yeah! That totally slipped my mind. Just give me two minutes.'

'Two minutes?' Jai laughed, 'Don't worry, take your time. We still have at least a couple of hours to go.'

Walking back to her hostel room, Megha recalled the events of the last hour. She had always liked Jai, but her respect for him had now increased immensely. Jai wanted to keep romance out of his life and Megha knew that, but she just couldn't get him out of her head. He had never let her down and in a sudden moment of clarity it seemed as if he was what she had been looking for all along.

'Raghu! Open up! Raghu!' Chris banged on the door loudly. He was impatient and the door had hardly opened before he fired away immediately, 'So brother, are you ready to receive the blessings of Damadam Mata? Maybe this year she'll shower some good luck on you.'

'Guess what? The first-year student has backed out and so I'll be conducting the puja again this year,' replied Raghu, adjusting his dhoti.

'Oh my, my, panditji. I am sure you are going to lose your virginity this year then. It's Mata's signal.'

The two chuckled and then, just like he had come, Chris hurried back, adding, 'Come soon. The Virgin Tree is waiting for you.'

Standing tall at the extreme end of the campus, the Virgin Tree was unlike any other. It was believed that anybody who took part in the puja on New Year's Eve would definitely lose their virginity the coming year. Therefore every year, on the last day of December, the puja organizers would pick a reigning female celebrity in Bollywood as the Damadam Mata and worship her at the Virgin Tree. The tree would be decorated with an assortment of things, including balloons, water-filled condoms and a poster of the fantasy queen of that year. It was Sunny Leone's turn this year and everyone gathered around the tree to seek blessings from the deity of love.

It was Ruhi's first time and having heard many stories about the puja, she couldn't wait for it to begin. Raghu being the panditji only added to her excitement. When he appeared on the scene wearing a dhoti, there immediately rose shouts of, '*Damadam Mata ki . . . jai! Damadam Mata ki . . . jai!*'

As Raghu began the puja, the shouts continued and some first-year students began playing the dhol. Everyone joined him in singing the *aarti* in hope of further impressing the love deity and earning her blessing. The excitement was contagious and everyone sang with great gusto. The third-year students kept a strict lookout for any sign of teachers, or as they liked to call them, *pyaar ke dushman*.

Once the aarti was over, Raghu offered an alcohol-soaked laddoo to the Mata, Sunny Leone, and then distributed the rest among the students. There was great cheer as the laddoos were consumed happily; then the condoms were burst, spraying water on everyone.

Seeing the water fall on Jai, Chris remarked, 'You got both the laddoo and the sprinkled water. You are going to get lucky very soon.'

Megha tried to hide her smile.

Jai laughed and replied, 'I wouldn't mind bursting each and every condom on your face.'

'You have Mata's blessings, don't waste it, Jai. Congratulations,' said Raghu, not wanting to miss the opportunity to make fun of his friend.

The fun and frolic continued and the puja was concluded with the tying of a holy red thread on the wrists of all the devoted followers. 'How do you feel, Mr Jai? You're going to get lucky this year,' Raghu continued mocking his friend.

'How do *you* feel, panditji? You've led the ceremony two years in a row. That's got to count for something,' Jai retorted.

Ruhi turned to Megha, 'I don't believe in any of these rituals, to be honest.'

'I am sure no one does. Most of them take part for the fun of it. They see it as a harmless exercise where everyone gets to hang out together and enjoy themselves,' Megha said.

'I agree. In any case, I don't really believe in college romance. It's nothing but infatuation, it has no real substance; on top of that, it distracts you from your other goals,' said Jai.

'And what exactly are these goals, Mr Bhakt?' Raghu asked.

'There's nothing in particular that I can think of at the moment. All I meant was that it is better to forge friendship and enjoy ourselves than to complicate things with a romantic relationship.'

'Love doesn't necessarily complicate things. If the relationship is genuine, the support you get may even help put you on the right track,' said Megha defensively.

'But in a relationship you are answerable for every single thing you do. You have to keep explaining yourself to your partner.'

'Plus, with you, I am sure girls will go mad with the dos and don'ts, including your *no drinking* status,' Raghu said looking at Jai.

Jai was a fitness freak. He led a healthy lifestyle and was of the opinion that everyone should treat their body with respect by eating right and exercising regularly.

'I am not the only one, there are hundreds of other people who don't smoke or drink,' he defended himself. 'Also, I don't go around giving fitness classes to everybody; I just think that everyone should take care of themselves by being healthy. There is nothing wrong in appreciating your body, right?'

'Anyway,' Ruhi butted in, putting a lid on the conversation, 'let's get back to work.'

The friends made their way to continue the Virgin Tree ritual. Students were directed to one end of the college ground where saplings were kept—each one was supposed to pick a sapling and plant it in the campus. After all the revelry earlier in the day, this was an effort to direct energies towards creating a sense of responsibility for the environment. Jai picked up two saplings and, following his lead, so did the others. Then they dug holes and put in their plants a little away from each other.

'This represents the seeds of our friendship,' Chris announced.

Smiles broke out on all the faces. As they carefully patted the soil around the saplings, Jai remarked, 'You know the best part of this exercise is that years from now, when a whole new batch of juniors enter the campus, they won't know who planted which tree. Regardless of caste, religion or race, they will all play under these trees and rest in their shade; and in turn, the trees will also shower them with endless love.'

'Yes, but if the roots are not strong enough, the tree may not be able to survive. Some trees, if not watered enough or protected from pests, may not grow to be as tall as the others. And that's where the discrimination arises. It all lies in our roots; if the roots are weak, the community will continue to be unstable,' Raghu commented in all seriousness.

'Do you have to argue against everything I say?' Jai laughed.

'I just can't help myself.'

'Are you guys done?' shouted Megha.

'I don't think we'll ever be done,' said Jai with a smile.

Having planted and watered the seeds of their friendship, they decided to celebrate it by welcoming the new year together. After much argument and friendly banter they finally managed to settle on a plan that pleased everyone. Isn't friendship strange? You might have different outlooks and opinions, but none of them seem to matter when you are together. You cherish your time with them, and while your troubles may not vanish, they certainly are not as painful in the company of your friends.

'Do you think they'll let us out? There are students guarding every gate,' said Chris.

'You don't need to worry about them. Is the SCI also involved in it?' Jai asked.

'Maybe,' replied Raghu.

Jai was not sure if Akhilesh, as the leader of the SCI, was the one stopping students from leaving the campus, but he was sure he had something to do with it. Even the students of AISC and their leader Krishna had ordered a ban on New Year's parties because of the petty crimes and rowdiness they usually led to. Only the ABCP had a neutral stand regarding such parties and they were Jai's ticket to leave the campus.

'The AISC and ABCP are constantly arguing with each other. But I'm on good terms with the ABCP, and have already informed them that I am going for a party outside the campus along with my friends. They agreed but said that the girls should be careful.'

'Is it safe?' Megha asked.

'When you are with us, you don't need to worry. As I said, a few representatives of the ABCP are good friends of mine. They won't let me down. I have supported them often in the past, even if it was indirectly.'

'Is that why you and Akhilesh argue so often these days?'

'That could be the reason. But I'm not really bothered about him; I am more worried about this guy Krishna. He has a good hold over his people and a strong political backup. We should be careful around them in case they try to pressure us into staying in by harassing the girls,' Jai suggested.

Ruhi, being new into this, looked worried, but was soon convinced by her friends that everything would be fine. Everyone then went to their respective rooms to rest and prepare for the evening ahead.

🎤

'See to it that no one leaves the gates of this campus. I'll beat you up along with the ones who do leave. The students have to be made to understand that it's for their own safety.'

Ruhi overheard Krishna addressing the representatives of the AISC while having her dinner in the canteen. Intrigued and scared, she strained her ears in an attempt to concentrate and listen to what they were saying. 'I want people at all the gates and extra security at the back gate,' continued Krishna.

Worried by Krishna's hostile tone, Ruhi rushed up to Megha's room. She desperately wanted to tell Megha what she had heard and anxiously banged on her door.

The door had barely been opened before Ruhi started speaking breathlessly, 'I overhead Krishna saying that he will not let anyone leave the campus tonight. He seemed very serious about it. I really hope Jai's plan doesn't backfire on us.'

'Calm down. If Jai says he is confident about something, you don't need to worry. He usually has some plan or the other. Also, he's a big guy around campus, no one messes with him,' Megha tried pacifying her friend.

Despite the comforting words, Ruhi was apprehensive. She had never experienced political agitation like this before and strongly considered staying on campus with her other friends from the social sciences department. But after some thinking, she changed her mind. She had rather enjoyed the past few days with Megha, who was from the same department, and her group of friends. She had become close to them but she knew that Raghu especially would feel let down if she were to back out. A little wary, a little curious and excited about the evening ahead, she went back to her room to get ready.

Jai banged on the bathroom door desperately to try and get Chris to come out. 'Chris, come on, we are getting late! The representatives of ABCP will be leaving the campus in some time.'

'So?'

'They are a very important part of our plan.'

'What exactly is the plan?' the door opened, revealing a grumpy-looking Chris, 'Relax, we still have time.'

'No, actually, we don't. Now get out, I need to use the bathroom,' Jai said, rushing past Chris to get ready. When he came out of the bathroom, Chris was sitting on the bed, playing a game on his mobile phone. Exasperated, Jai grabbed the phone from his hand and told him to start packing the props and other things for the party. He did as he was told, but soon plonked on a chair to read a magazine. Jai looked at him unhappily and then gave up. *It's better if I do the rest by myself*, he thought.

Suddenly, a knock. Alarmed because they were not ready yet, Jai opened the door, expecting the ABCP members. He was relieved to find Raghu and the girls instead. He hurriedly resumed his work and shouted at Chris to get changed.

'Is everything going according to plan?' Megha asked.

'Of course,' replied Jai, running a comb through his hair.

Everyone was ready, including Ruhi, who had long forgotten her worries at the prospect of partying all night.

They headed towards the back gate of the campus where the ABCP representatives were supposed to gather. Raghu was a little anxious about taking their help since he didn't agree with their ideology. But what mattered at the moment was to be able to leave the campus safely, so he remained silent. When they reached the gate, they were greeted by the ABCP representatives.

'You don't need to worry. The AISC won't dare touch you when you are with us,' said one of the representatives.

'We don't want to get involved in any fight with them, there are girls with us,' Jai declared.

'Leave it to us. They just pretend to care about the safety of women, when most of them are actually hooligans. We are here to help you but don't make us regret it by getting involved in any illegal activity. Come back on time. It'll be safe to enter because soon everyone will get involved in their own celebrations,' said another of Jai's friends. 'If there's any problem, I will give you a call.'

'Sure.'

The group was joined by one of the senior professors of the college and the plan slowly unfolded. The professor was leaving town and students of the ABCP were dropping him off at the Nizamuddin railway station. Jai and his gang were to mingle and appear to be a part of that group, and then go their own way.

'These students . . .'

The professor was about to inquire about Jai and his friends when a member of the ABCP who was on good terms with the professor intervened, 'They are heading to a close relative's home to celebrate the new year.'

'A relative?' the professor asked sceptically.

'Trust me, sir. I wouldn't lie.'

'Yes, sir, my uncle stays close by and has invited us to spend some time with him. We were supposed to go in the morning but he got late at work and asked us to come now,' Jai explained. 'So when I heard that you were leaving campus I asked if we could join you because it wouldn't be safe for the girls otherwise. I hope you don't mind, sir.'

'Hmm,' the professor seemed to agree.

With that, Jai knew no one could stop the car of a professor who was leaving town.

'You all sit in that car,' Jai's friend said to them.

An Innova was parked behind the college Ambassador that the professor was to travel in. A couple of representatives got into the car carrying the professor, while the others boarded the Innova with Jai and his friends. As they reached the main gate, the professor rolled down the window of the Ambassador and ordered the gate to be opened. The AISC students standing near the security guards did not suspect a thing and allowed the cars to pass.

Seeing Ruhi smile with relief, Megha winked at her. Her fear was left behind, locked inside the gates of the campus.

The moment the car dropped them at their destination, Raghu and Chris shouted with excitement. The journey of life has lots to offer, but without friends the path seems dull and lonely. Elated, the friends congratulated each other on their accomplishment and hugged each other with joy. Carefree and electrified, their party had just begun.

Four

20 May 2016

'How could you even think something like that, Raghu? I still can't believe you feel that way,' said Chris, giving him a surprised look.

'Why, what did I say wrong? Isn't it all because of these people? Why were only both of us made to suffer while he escaped without any repercussions?' Raghu shouted, looking accusingly at Jai.

'It was never about me. It was nobody's fault and we couldn't have helped what happened. But please, don't drag me into this,' Jai said fiercely.

'Raghu, are you in your senses?' Ruhi tried to calm him down.

'I am . . . I know what I am talking about. He has always disagreed with me—these bhakts are shameless creatures. They can never understand our pain.'

'When did it come down to this? Yours and mine? That too on the basis of caste?'

'It has been like this for a long time. Ever since you started treating us like we didn't exist, since you started harassing us and what not,' said Raghu. 'Chris, it'd be better if you realize what is happening soon. Otherwise you will be termed as an adarsh liberal by these bhakts and they will snatch your identity. Instead of arguing with me, you should ask him what he thinks about our existence.'

'You're going too far, Raghu. We're all friends here. Calm down and think about what you are accusing me of,' Jai said, trying to pacify Raghu.

Megha was speechless with shock at how Raghu and Jai were turning against each other. She knew that Jai had done nothing wrong but had no clue how to make Raghu understand that. Jai genuinely thought of Raghu as a close friend, but recent events had turned things sour between them. Sitting outside the canteen, everyone watched the drama unfold.

'This is not you talking, I'm sure someone else has put these words into your mouth. Remember I told you once that anyone can manipulate you?' added Jai.

'Do you think I have no opinions of my own? Do you think I can't stand up for my own rights? I will show you!' Raghu exclaimed.

Just before he could punch Jai, Chris intervened and pushed Raghu aside. It was bizarre that things had come to such an ugly turn between two close friends. Convinced that his strange behaviour was somebody else's doing, the rest of the friends tried reasoning with Raghu, but with little effect.

'Fuck off!' Jai shouted in anger. He had believed that they were best friends, and Raghu's harsh words cut deep.

In life, humans can deal with a great amount of loss and still regain their confidence, but the falling out of friends is the greatest loss of all.

Five

13 June 2016

True to his word, Krishna officially welcomed the student and gave him a number of tasks, which he executed with ease. He quickly became one of Krishna's favourites. Though he was not made to travel again, he controlled and managed the tasks assigned to people by the higher authorities. However, the experience of his first task— when everything seemed covert and suspicious—was always there in a corner of his mind, making him feel a little uncertain about his environment all the time.

There seemed to be a strong dissonance between how things ought to be carried out and how they actually were. The seeds of doubt flourished due to the lack of information provided to him, and although he completed all his tasks faithfully, his worrying thoughts led him to feel guilty. Most of the time, however, he managed to quieten his thoughts as there was no substantial proof of any wrong or illegal activity.

'We have a task we need to complete,' Krishna said to the newest members of his movement, Kraanti. The student was also associated with the AISC. 'Our boxes have arrived and need to be delivered.'

Pointing at the same student, he added, 'He will guide you and tell you all the details.'

The student had hoped he would get to see the bigger picture and clear all the doubts he had, but nothing was clarified as Krishna simply explained that there was a shipment of literature books coming from across the border.

The task went smoothly and the books were not only collected in a timely fashion, but were also delivered in good condition. Even then, the student could not shake off a nagging feeling that someone was watching him, and this kept him on his toes constantly. Each time a task was assigned, a cold feeling of doubt would creep over him, and he would breathe easy only on the confirmation of the success of the task. On one such occasion, he headed towards Krishna to inform him of the good news.

'Well done, my boy. You are turning out to be a real asset to our wing,' Krishna said.

'Thank you.' The blanket of questions still weighed heavily on him.

'Don't thank me. We are here to make sure that people from our caste do not suffer,' the student leader said as he came and sat near him on the table.

'Yes.'

'Why should we constantly live with the fear of being ostracized or treated as inferior? One doesn't realize the depth of such humiliation until he has faced it. But you have experienced it and you know exactly how it feels, right?'

He nodded, only partially convinced, and left for the day.

As he opened the door of his room, he saw a letter on the floor. He locked the door behind him quickly and picked up the envelope. His name was written in bold letters.

We value your contribution towards Kraanti, MR RAGHU.

He tore open the envelope and began to read the letter.

To my favourite student Raghu,
You have proven to be a great asset to Kraanti and we
appreciate your contribution towards the betterment
of people from the lower castes. We hope you will
continue to serve our organization.
Student leader of AISC,
Krishna

Raghu kept the letter aside and thought how different his life was now. Unsure about how to proceed, he wished he knew more about the organization and the work they were doing. Despite honestly completing the tasks he was given, Raghu was unaware that a large part of the world he had stepped into was nothing but an illusion!

Six

1 January 2016

The year on the calendar had changed. It was almost noon but the campus remained silent on the first day of the new year. The first of January should be officially declared as Hangover Day. A few go through food hangovers while the rest experience alcohol hangovers. Chris and the others belonged to the latter category while Jai fit into the former.

As he sat sipping his tea slowly and reading the newspaper in the café, an article about their college caught Jai's attention. The place was almost empty and in between reading the piece, he saw Chris walking towards him.

'Happy new year,' Jai greeted him.

'Same to you,' Chris responded dryly, his hangover evident.

'Did you read the news?'

'What news? That *Dilwale* managed to collect higher collections than *Bajirao* yesterday?' The movie buff in him that idolized SRK shone through the horrible hangover. He eagerly took a seat.

'No, I'm talking about the professors who were stopped from entering the campus last night after we left. They said it was because of some differences in social ideology.'

'Seriously? Who was behind it?'

'Krishna. Who else?'

'That's ridiculous.'

'Yes and one of the professors got into a fight with the security guards who denied him entry,' Jai said, drinking the last of the tea.

'You want some more tea?' Chris asked, getting up to place an order, while Jai continued reading the news.

'No, thanks.'

'But I must say . . . last night was crazy. You saw that chick who was dancing with me? She almost kissed me.' Chris sighed.

'I am sure she did much more than that in your fantasies.'

'Jai Damadam Mata!' Chris shouted, evoking the Virgin Tree slogan.

They both laughed. Chris mulled over asking Jai about Megha. The way Megha kept glancing at him the previous night made it pretty clear that she liked him. Chris wanted to find out the other side of the story.

'You saw Megha yesterday?'

'Yesterday? I have been seeing her every day since first year,' Jai said, putting the newspaper aside.

'Not in that sense. But in *that* sense.'

'Which sense?' Jai rolled his eyes.

'Come on . . . she was totally into you yesterday. '

Jai ignored him and picked up the newspaper again.

Chris threw it aside and exclaimed, 'I am asking you something!'

'You already know what my answer is. I'm not looking for a relationship right now. I'm not saying that she's not my type or that she's not attractive, but I just don't feel the same way.'

'She loves you Jai, truly loves you. That's rare.'

'It takes a lot of effort to be in a relationship. To handle the egos, to devote your time and to keep each other constantly updated about your whereabouts. Just the thought of it makes me feel caged. I am not saying all relationships are like this, I have a number of friends who are in committed, happy relationships. It's just that I am not mentally prepared for one right now, and I'm sure she isn't either.'

Jai was very clear about his feelings and didn't want to ruin his friendship with Megha. He respected her emotions and the way she felt but didn't think it was worth the risk. Chris liked Jai's outspoken attitude. Had it been someone else, they might have played with Megha's emotions, but not Jai. He believed in keeping his relationships transparent.

'That's exactly what I love about you,' expressed Chris. 'Never change.'

'That's last night's alcohol speaking.' Jai laughed.

'Oh please. I'm not drunk any more.' Chris laughed along.

Their conversation continued, rolling over New Year's resolutions, girls in the college, politics and campus diaries, fuelled by endless cups of tea. It finally came to a halt when they spotted Ruhi and Raghu walking out of the gate, engrossed in each other. Ruhi was smiling while looking at Raghu's hand gestures; it seemed like he was telling her a story. Jai and Chris didn't disturb them, and the couple didn't bother stopping by either.

'I am sure there is something cooking between them.'

'Did you drink vodka yesterday?' Jai asked suspiciously. 'Why?'

'You have started behaving like a girl, constantly gossiping.' Jai smirked.

'I just wanted to know what you thought.'

'You have nothing better to do than talk about everyone else's lives. You are like my grandma who keeps an account of the entire colony.'

But Chris persisted. 'Of course there's something going on, there's no doubt about it,' Jai finally said. 'We all know Raghu's crazy about her and I think Ruhi might feel the same way now. The only thing that worries me is that Ruhi is a Brahmin and Raghu is from a lower caste.'

'How does that matter? If two people love each other, such things become meaningless. Who the hell believes in all this nonsense anyway?' Chris said.

'It doesn't matter to me, but I hope it doesn't become a concern for Ruhi in the future, when the parents get involved. Also, she loves all kinds of animals, while Raghu loves *eating* all kinds of animals,' Jai responded.

After their discussion about almost everything, they decided to call it a day. Jai and Chris got along well and though they never spoke about it, they knew they were special to each other. Having been through a lot together, their relationship was honest and transparent, with both of them supporting each other—whenever the situation demanded it.

Raghu stretched his sore limbs and let out a groan when his gaze trailed lazily to his phone, which was blaring out its usual alarm. While silencing it he saw there was a message from Ruhi. He felt a shiver of excitement as he tapped it open, *Are you awake? Everyone is sleeping and I am getting bored. Any plans?*

Raghu was on cloud nine; it was the first day of the year and hopefully his first date if he played his cards right.

No plans, let's go out for lunch? Raghu messaged.

Cool, I'll see you in five, came her prompt reply.

Despite his grogginess Raghu rushed into the washroom and even in the freezing cold, managed to pour a bucket of water over himself.

No one puts himself through freezing torture as this right after New Year's Eve unless he has a date lined up, he thought to himself as he dried off.

Ruhi, who was ready and waiting, got impatient after fifteen minutes of silence and messaged Raghu again, *If it's going to take more time, then it's OK, just leave it. I don't mind.*

Raghu read it and cursed himself. He rushed out of the room without even tying his shoelaces, while typing frantically.

I am waiting for you downstairs; I thought you weren't ready yet.

A little relieved at not seeing Ruhi waiting for him, he bent down to tie his shoelaces.

'Ready?' he heard her say. She stood behind him, putting her phone into her bag.

'Of course.'

'Last night is just a blur for me. Chris persuaded me to drink and I stupidly tried to keep up with him. He was able to tolerate his alcohol while I acted like a complete fool.'

Ruhi laughed. 'And before you passed out you blurted out something about having a crush on me?'

Raghu felt a rush of embarrassment. *I need to get my shit together*, he thought, as his stomach knotted up in nervous anticipation.

'Were you being serious?' Ruhi asked softly.

There was silence for the next few seconds, as they both waited for the other to speak.

'You know that day it was actually my idea to throw stones at that dog,' Raghu confessed. 'Later I felt so guilty that I asked Megha to take the blame. Can you forgive me? I promise I won't do it again, it wasn't even intentional. Trust me.'

'Why did you lie then?'

'I didn't. I just told Megha to go and stop you because . . .'

'Because what?'

'Nothing.'

'Come on.' Ruhi rolled her eyes at him.

'I didn't want to lose you . . . your friendship, I mean. You know how it is. At that moment I panicked and didn't know what to do. But otherwise I am not that cruel, especially towards dogs. They are so cute.'

Ruhi smiled as they walked past the main gate. Both of them were so engrossed that they didn't notice Jai and Chris sitting at the café and observing them keenly.

'So why are you telling me the truth now?'

'It's one of my New Year's resolutions. Not to lie.' Raghu chuckled.

'I appreciate it. But these resolutions usually don't last very long. It's just like buying a new phone; you are very careful with it the first few days, and after a while you just fling it around without a care.'

'No, I am serious about this one . . .' Raghu tried hard to fight his case. Lost in each other's company, they didn't realize how much they had walked until they reached the restaurant they were supposed to eat in. The taxi ride was not required after all.

'You are adorable.' Ruhi smiled as they entered the restaurant.

'Veg or non-veg?' Raghu asked, flipping through the menu. Almost immediately he realized his mistake, 'Oh . . . I am sorry.'

'What if, one day, you have to give up non-vegetarian food? Will you be able to?'

'Um . . .'

'You know that I am a Brahmin, right?'

'Yes, do you know what I am?'

'I do, but I don't care. As a person, you are adorable.'

In his head, Raghu broke out into a victory dance, his spirit soared until he realized that Ruhi's words could contain an unspoken 'but'.

'What I asked earlier was a serious question.'

At first his brain refused to comprehend what she was actually saying, but eventually her words sunk in and he wanted to crawl under the table and hide.

Raghu thought for a while and decided to go all in. His gaze kept flitting between the white plates on the table and the ceiling fan above. Apprehensively, he tugged at a loose thread on the sleeve of his shirt and said, 'I'll try to be more adorable by giving up non-vegetarian food.' He lifted his chin in an attempt to appear more confident.

'Is that also one of your New Year's resolutions?' Ruhi was smiling now.

'Certainly.'

'Liar.'

After paying their bill at the café, Jai and Chris went outside the campus, to a dhaba nearby. Though it was noon, there was still a chill in the air, giving the day a gloomy feel. Jai wanted to meet his friend from ABCP who had helped them the previous day. After hearing about the professors who had been prevented from entering the campus, he realized how lucky they had been and wanted to thank his friend for the smooth execution of the plan. He also wanted to check on Megha, as her persistent migraine had given her some trouble at the party as well.

Just as they were returning to the campus, Jai saw the same hooligans who had been troubling Megha the previous day.

'Chris, these are the same bastards who were following Megha . . .'

Leaving the rest of the sentence hanging, Jai started sprinting towards the group. Chris tried to follow him, but his hangover slowed him down. On seeing Jai charging towards them, the group sped away on their bikes. Jai stopped and tried to catch his breath as Chris finally caught up with him.

'Did you see where they came from?'

'No. But they went in that direction,' Jai said, pointing towards the lane that turned left after leaving the university gates.

He took a deep breath and tried to analyse where they could have come from. He was still in deep thought when they walked back towards the campus.

'I am not going to spare them,' he finally declared.

'Chill. We won't. But let me ask you one thing; if you care about Megha, why don't you . . . ?' Chris's voice trailed off.

'I can't care about her as a friend?'

'Of course you can.' Chris laughed.

No matter what he said, Jai refused to fall for his tricks. Finally Chris gave up and went to his room to sleep.

Meanwhile, Jai called Megha outside and within minutes, she was at the back gate of the campus.

'I saw them again,' Jai said as Megha approached him.

'The bikers?' she asked, tying her hair into a ponytail.

'Yes. I am not going to leave those bastards alone. I hate people who try to show dominance over girls by tormenting them.' Jai's anger was reflected in his words.

Megha, however, didn't show any such reaction and started fiddling with her phone to show him pictures from the previous night.

'Is your headache better now?'

Megha nodded and showed him a couple of their pictures she wanted to upload on Facebook. She looked up from her phone and found him standing close. His arm was grazing hers and for a moment she wished she could throw hers around him without any fear of his reaction. 'I think this one looks good. My nose looks amazing here.' Jai winked.

'And my pout too.'

'Without a doubt.'

They both looked at each other in silence for a second, before looking away. 'Are you attending any classes today?' Jai asked, changing the topic.

'No, Ruhi will take notes for me.'

'You better start attending from tomorrow before the professors get suspicious and start spying on you. Today, just take your medicines and rest for a while,' Jai advised as he started walking towards the lecture hall.

Megha continued to look at him as he walked away from her. If the only way to stay close to him was pretending not to like him, then she'd do that. But the attraction she felt for him could not be ignored; she just couldn't stop staring at his muscular, well-built body. She knew Jai was a caring soul who loved his friends, but he was also mysterious, and never opened up about his feelings to anyone. Megha was unsure whether her feelings for Jai represented her true love for him or if she was simply lusting after his body.

She was still sitting at the same spot, uploading a few photos from the party, when Akhilesh approached her.

'Don't tell me you're uploading another one of those articles,' he said sarcastically.

'What's your problem? Why do you keep troubling me?'

'I thought I made it clear the other day,' he said, sitting down beside her.

Megha immediately got up and glared at him, 'What?'

'I love you. You heard me when I said that, right? You thought I was just trying to prove my point and completely ignored my feelings,' he said while spreading his arms across the bench and folding up his legs comfortably. He was completely at ease, unfazed by Megha's fury.

'You have gone mad. I am not going to delete any posts,' said Megha starting to leave.

'I am not asking you to delete it today; rather I am asking you to write a letter. A love letter from Akhilesh to Megha . . . You are such a good writer.'

'Fuck off.'

'Fine. Then I will write it, hand it over to you and you will be able to read it. Isn't that such a waste of time, when you could simply write it so well yourself?'

On seeing Megha's stony face he continued, 'You don't have to post it on Facebook . . . I don't mind.'

'Get a life,' said Megha, turning to leave.

Akhilesh watched her leave with a wicked smile on his face.

Megha knew that he just wanted to upset her but she didn't want to get into an argument and spoil her mood so soon after meeting Jai. She wished she could tell the difference between love and infatuation. Jai, on the other hand, wanted to focus on his college activities and wasn't going to let love come in the way, despite Chris's numerous attempts to distract him. Raghu alone was not only sure about his feelings but was ready to take the plunge with Ruhi.

Ruhi too somewhere hid her feelings for him. Strange are the equations of life and love, where it is never simple to draw one straight line between two points.

Seven

26 January 2016

'It has been more than two weeks since Mani—a student of MGU—mysteriously disappeared from the campus grounds following a brutal assault by a group of students belonging to AISC,' read the front-page story of a leading newspaper on 26 January.

'A student vanished from a campus in Delhi after being thrashed by members of an organization linked to the president of the student union. This event is ominous and disturbing,' said another.

'University campuses and hostels are dens for petty crime and corrupt politicians; their dark corridors are lit by tales of point-blank shootings and intense rivalries between two or more contending groups.'

And it continued.

Every newspaper had the story of the missing MGU student on their front page. The student, Mani from Madurai, had gone missing after the SCI protests against New Year celebrations and the prevention of professors from entering the college. A few students, as well as the hostel authorities, had information about his disappearance, but they chose to remain silent.

For more than two weeks, there was no progress by the Delhi Police, leading Akhilesh and the SCI to contact the media. Each time Krishna, the leader of the AISC, was interrogated, he had only one thing to say—'We are not involved in the case.' Akhilesh claimed that if the student had been from north India, the case would have been given much more importance, but since the student was from the south, there was no sense of urgency and the police remained ineffective.

After the disappearance, different loyalties came to light—the most surprising one being that of the ABCP. They usually opposed anything related to both the SCI and the AISC, but in the case of the missing student, they sprang into action and compelled the police to move quickly.

'On the night of our campaign, Mani slapped a student of AISC who came into his room. The issue was then taken to the warden of the hostel who advised Mani to shift to another room. After shifting, Mani even apologized to the student he slapped, but the next morning, he was nowhere to be found. Doesn't this indicate a clear and strong involvement of the AISC in Mani's disappearance?' Akhilesh addressed a huge mob that had gathered inside the campus.

On the other side of the campus, AISC students gathered to hear Krishna's side of the story.

'Our student said that he was slapped and Mani admitted to that as well. When Mani was being taken to the warden, he was attacked by other parties like the ABCP and there were some comments about his religious identity as well.'

The propaganda continued all around the campus. The place where students had taken admission to gain knowledge and to learn the values of life had now became a war zone of clashing political agendas. All the parties stood against each other and the intellectual structure of the great institution seemed to be crumbling. In the battle between AISC and SCI, ABCP kept silent, although they were hoping for violence and escalating tension between the groups. Jai asked Megha and Ruhi to stay indoors, while he, along with Raghu, Chris and the other students, went to witness the ongoing chaos.

'What's ABCP's take on all this?' Chris asked Jai, while Raghu pretended not to look too interested.

'They are just supporting the search for the student. They didn't have any problem with him and are definitely not involved in his kidnapping. They have always believed in true nationalism rather than the kind of wars that the AISC fight—those that are based on caste and religion.' Jai sounded confident since he was good friends with a number of ABCP members. 'I don't know how these students can be so opposed to members of another religion. It's really strange to see this scenario in modern India and especially among those of our generation.'

After pausing for a moment, he continued, 'The leaders of these parties are storytellers. They have the power to brainwash your thinking process and your ideologies. Even if you spend just a few days with them, your entire outlook towards life will change. They manipulate people on the grounds of religion and caste, creating more barriers than the ones they are trying to break.'

'Anyway,' Chris intervened, trying to change the topic, 'Raghu, did you stop eating meat? I am planning to have some today.'

'You people are cruel . . . I am trying.'

Jai piped up to Raghu's rescue, 'Chris, you should respect what he is doing. His New Year's resolution has lasted for almost twenty-five days. That's a real achievement for someone who used to eat so much meat.'

'So the moral of the story is that love changes a person,' Chris said in mock seriousness.

'Yeah, tried and tested; with a disclaimer of twenty-five days,' Jai said as they walked out of the campus to get something to eat.

Raghu couldn't stop smiling. How easily their charged discussion just a few minutes back on political ideologies had evaporated! Friends can lighten any situation no matter what the circumstances. And so, despite the chaos in the campus, the three friends remained insulated in their friendship.

I hate this conflicted state of mind, my eyes desperately searching for some clarity among these jumbled words and the throbbing ache in my head. I seem to be hopelessly lost; not only in love, but in all aspects of my life.

Megha typed out her status and stared blankly at the screen of her mobile phone. A message from Ruhi popped up; she was coming to meet her. Megha continued writing her post:

What scares me is that I cannot differentiate between true feelings and the ghost of my emotions. When I look into the mirror, I see a stranger. Who am I, I ask. There are no answers but only endless questions.

I get a strange sense of satisfaction watching the words disappear letter by letter as I hold down the backspace key. Sometimes it feels like that is the perfect example of real life. Someone out there is holding down my backspace key and the longer he does this, the more I disappear. I try to write my story again but there he is, erasing, deleting. We are all just pieces in life's game of chess. Methodically, it seems to place us where it needs us, only to play a risky game, where we are sacrificed for the benefit of someone else. Caught between the virtual and the real world, I try to find my true reflection, where the weight of my emotions lie. Isn't that strange? We think we are the ones living this life but it is actually life that pulls all the strings.

'Megha! Megha!'

There was a knock at the door. Megha clicked on the status icon to post her thoughts online and got up to open the door.

'Why is your phone not reachable? I have been trying to call you for so long!' Ruhi exclaimed.

Megha checked the signal on her phone; there was no dip in strength. 'No clue. Maybe I need to change my service provider; this happens quite a lot these days.'

'Anyway, where is Jai?'

Somewhere in my Facebook post, thought Megha.

'How would I know?' she said out loud. 'Why?'

'Akhilesh is up to something again. Some new drama in the campus over the missing student . . .'

'I am sure that's not what you came here to talk to me about. What's the matter?'

'I don't know how to say this . . .' Ruhi sat on the bed, folding her legs.

'Is it about Raghu?'

Ruhi blushed. 'Honestly, I've been in a number of relationships before. After the first one, none of them have been very serious. The first guy I dated played with my emotions and left me heartbroken; because of that experience I didn't want to feel vulnerable again, and have never really opened up to a guy.'

'So what are you trying to say? Why this preface?' said Megha, offering Ruhi some chips.

'No, thanks.' She continued, 'At first I was confused about Raghu. I really didn't know what I wanted, if my feelings for him were actually serious.'

That's exactly how I feel about Jai.

Ruhi went on, 'So, I decided to be friends with him first and find out what he is really like. He seems really nice and there are some things about him that I adore. In the beginning I had my doubts, but he's been honest with me lately and seems to be genuinely interested in me. The only thing that worries me now are our castes and whether we can really have a future together.'

'First, do you love him?' Megha asked, coming straight to the point.

'Ummm . . . It's like . . .'

'Yes or no?'

'Yes.'

'Then why are you worried about his caste? You don't live in some rural area where the panchayat decides who you should marry. You live in a big city and more importantly, you are capable of making independent decisions. If you are sure about your feelings, don't let unimportant things like caste get in the way.'

'You are right, but it's never that easy.'

'I never said it was easy, but if your feelings are genuine, then it's worth it. Did he say something?'

'His New Year's resolution is to stop eating non-vegetarian food. "I'll try," he says,' Ruhi said, mimicking Raghu's panicked tone.

Megha couldn't stop laughing, 'Sometimes I forget what an idiot he can be.'

'He surely is,' Ruhi said with fondness.

'You should tell him that the day he kisses a chicken, he can't kiss you. After that you'll see him wandering around only pure vegetarian restaurants.'

Raghu became the target and the girls kept firing bullets his way. Moving on to the next victim, Ruhi inquired about Jai. 'We are friends. Nothing more than that.'

'You spend so much time together, you never fell for him?'

'I don't know. Maybe like you, even I'm not looking for something very serious.'

It's incredible how unsure we are of particular feelings. One moment the feeling is so real, and the next it's vanished. With no idea where these emotions come from and where they go, it is these inexplicable moments that make life magical.

I know she will say yes, I am sure she will. She has to . . . Okay, but what if she says no? But why will she? No, she won't. I love her. I am sure no one can love her more than I do. But does she love me? But why wouldn't she . . . ?

Raghu's heart and mind battled against each other as a hundred different thoughts flooded him. He wanted to scream out his love for Ruhi, but the words kept getting caught in his throat. Half-formed sentences would die away and awkward silences prevail when he was with her.

Ruhi's emotions were no different. Sitting in one corner of her room, playing with her hair, she kept thinking about the future. She stared down at her trembling hands and for the first time realized the depth of her emotions.

It was two in the morning and Raghu kept staring at Ruhi's display picture on WhatsApp.

'Still online?' A messaged popped up on his phone.

He froze as anticipation pumped through his veins. *Wow, was she also stalking me?*

'Reading a book,' he replied casually.

After a few minutes of silence, he messaged her again. 'Did you see my Snapchat?'

'No,' came the instant reply.

'Have a look.'

Ruhi opened her Snapchat and looked for Raghu's post.

I'm in love with you, and I'm not in the business of denying myself the simple pleasure of saying things which are true.

He had highlighted a line from some novel and uploaded a picture of the page.

Ruhi read the line again. Was this a personal message for her? Or just a line from some book he had read? She got the hint, but continued to respond casually.

'Nice quote. Is it from a new book you're reading?'

'Yes. As a reader you should understand the depth of the quote.'

'By reader do you mean the person reading the novel or the ones reading your Snapchat story?'

Raghu had a smile on his face; his attempt to woo her through social media was paying off. 'Have you read *The Fault in Our Stars* by John Green?' he asked her.

Is she deliberately taking a long time to reply to my messages or am I just overthinking it?

'No. I am done with those love stories,' Ruhi typed finally. She tried to avoid the topic deliberately, although she was reading a love story herself.

'And why is that so? They aren't that boring,' Raghu pushed on.

At least when you are in it, he thought to himself.

'It's just that they are so predictable.'

'I don't think so. Can you predict ours?'

Before Raghu realized what he had said, he had hit Send.

His true feelings were out in the open and there was nothing he could do to take his words back.

Ruhi tried to call Raghu but all she heard was the mechanized voice saying the number was switched off.

Raghu wanted to bite his tongue. He had never meant to send that message, it had come out as a reflexive response to her words. Ruhi on the other side of the phone wanted to clear the air and speak to him directly instead of playing hide-and-seek with their emotions. She tried calling him a couple of times more before she decided to leave a message.

It's not that easy; you know what I am talking about. I've seen the tears on people's faces, the hearts breaking due to simple misunderstandings. You know better than anyone the distance between us when it comes to our families. I am not talking about our upbringing but about the mindset that surrounds us everywhere we go. Everything is decided by our parents; the boy, the girl, the date, the marriage. It takes a lot of courage to have a love marriage. I have seen loveless souls walking around, burdened by the decisions of their parents and families. I don't know how this will ever work. But I have read The Fault in Our Stars. ☺

Ruhi put her phone to charge and went to sleep.

After an hour or so, Raghu dared to switch on his phone and Ruhi's WhatsApp message immediately popped up. He mulled over it for a while and with an optimistic approach decided to take the next step. He knew that it was never easy to go up to the person you love and tell them how you feel, but he couldn't risk losing Ruhi to the arms of another boy. Half the love stories in this world end before they can even begin because people are too scared to express their emotions, too scared of the rejection that they think might follow. Raghu still wasn't completely confident, so he thought of another way to express his love. He ran off to the campus, trying to avoid meeting anyone he knew.

'Where are you heading? You seem to be in a great rush,' Chris called out when he saw Raghu climbing up the staircase that led to the staff room.

'I'll talk to you later. Do you have any idea where Ruhi is?'

'I think she's in the canteen, why?' he asked curiously.

'Nothing,' Raghu replied instantly, and avoiding further questions, hurried off.

Intrigued, Chris followed him to the staff room. But Raghu did not stop there. He climbed further up the stairs until he reached the college studio. There Chris saw him talking to the person in charge and handing over some money. Confident that something was not right, Chris took the lift to the ground floor and reached the canteen. It was early morning and only a few chairs were occupied; most students were in class. He spotted Ruhi sitting with the others and hurried towards them.

'Raghu is up to something.'

'What happened?' Ruhi asked.

'I saw him giving some money to . . .' Chris's voice trailed off. He took a deep breath and sat down next to Jai.

'Giving money to whom? Is everything fine?'

'I don't know. I saw Raghu giving some money to the studio in-charge.'

'What? Why did he do that?' asked Megha surprised.

Ruhi looked at the messages they had exchanged the previous night. There were no clues there.

As they tried to comprehend Raghu's bizarre behaviour, they suddenly heard his voice boom all around them.

'Ruhi . . . it's me,' Raghu's voice was loud and clear through the college loudspeakers, used by the campus radio recording studio. 'I don't know how you will react to this, but I have to say it. I can't keep this a secret any longer.' He didn't mention his name; Ruhi would know who it was.

'Ruhi . . . you are my Hazel. Hazel from *The Fault in Our Stars*. I hope you know what I mean when I say this. I am not dying. I just wanted to say that . . . I have tasted love. I taste it every day. When I look at you, when I talk to you, everything you do makes me fall more in love. For a long time, I couldn't understand why you were so special to me, but after the time we spent together I no longer have to wonder. It's everything, everything you do, everything about you is special. Sometimes when I can't bear to be away from you, I call you and hang up, afraid of what you will say. Even now I am afraid of what your reaction will be. But every time I close my eyes, I see you, your hair falling on your shoulders, the way you smile, the sound of your laugh. If I focus hard enough I can picture you standing beside me. But picturing you is not enough. It's never enough. I want to be next to you right now. I want to look at your hands in mine. I want to know everything about you. I love you, Ruhi.'

Ruhi listened without a word. The whole college did. After some time, Raghu came down the stairs nervously, excited to meet her, but afraid of being apprehended by professors or other members of the staff. The moment he reached the canteen door, he saw Ruhi, sitting with the others. She was stunned, unable to believe what had just happened.

It was buzzing all around and yet, when their eyes met, their surroundings melted away in a blur. The romantic tension was evident in the way they walked towards each other; Ruhi blushed as the distance lessened and she came face-to-face with Raghu.

'I am sure it's every Ruhi's dream for something like this to happen to her,' she said. 'Let them keep dreaming, I belong only to you. I want to reach out to you, touch you, and hear you say that you love me.'

'I know, your eyes have always told me the truth, even if you were too scared to say it. I also want to feel your arms around me and feel safe, protected from everything.'

'Don't worry. I'll always be there and together we will face whatever obstacle comes our way.'

Love is often mistaken to be a simple emotion, but it's not. It's an incredibly personal feeling often mistaken for sheer ecstasy. When pure, love can be the bond between two souls and that is what Raghu and Ruhi became in that moment—two bodies with one soul.

Eight

Ruhi and Raghu had found a breath of fresh air in a city blanketed with smog. Ruhi had suppressed her feelings for Raghu, but after his declaration they broke loose like a tidal wave. He was like a sprouting seed that indicated new beginnings for her while she was the spark that illuminated the darkened gateways to his soul. The good mood spilled over on to Jai, Megha and Chris, who were also overjoyed at their friends' new-found love. Megha couldn't stop congratulating the couple, while Chris attributed the love to Damadam Mata's blessing.

'I have an idea.' Ruhi grinned slyly, and Raghu's eyes opened wide in understanding. 'No way, Ruhi,' Raghu said, shaking his head disbelievingly. 'Yes way, come on,' Ruhi announced as they got up to leave.

Around midnight the same day, both Raghu and Ruhi were itching to see each other, despite spending the whole day together. Caught up in the excitement of the whirlwind love affair, Ruhi cooked up a plan to sneak into the boys' hostel. She called Raghu. A few boys' wings had a common mess for both boys and girls, so the plan was to gain entry through that.

'You want to sneak into the boys' hostel, and that too at midnight? Are you serious?' Raghu asked incredulously.

'I'm more than serious. It's not a big deal. Girls are allowed in the common mess though boys aren't allowed to enter the girls' hostel. So let me take advantage of that and enter yours.'

'Are you planning to get me murdered?' Raghu couldn't believe Ruhi actually wanted to take such a risk.

'No, now put the phone down and open the door when I get there.'

The only thing Ruhi was worried about was being seen by students of the AISC or SCI, but everything went smoothly and soon she was standing outside Raghu's door.

Raghu opened the door quietly, 'You shouldn't have taken this risk.'

Ruhi didn't bother to reply and planted a kiss on his lips. As their tongues swirled together, Raghu's nervousness evaporated and he held her tight. They continued to kiss each other, until both of them were gasping for breath.

'It's not as bad as I expected,' Ruhi said, scanning the room.

'What did you expect?'

'I expected at least a couple of your boxers lying around, that too unwashed, with holes in them.' She laughed.

'Isn't that a very sexist thought? That girls are clean and tidy while guys are messy?' Raghu asked as he placed a cup on the induction stove.

'Do you even know how to cook or are you just showing off?' she asked.

'Oh please, I am a good cook. That's why I prefer to keep an induction stove and a mini refrigerator despite paying for the mess food.'

Raghu showed her the refrigerator which contained a few vegetables and some frozen chicken.

'Let's make something then,' Ruhi suggested.

'Sure, how about rajma? I already have some soaked.'

'Great. Let me help you,' she said, getting up from the bed and walking towards him.

But Raghu warned, 'Don't come near the stove.'

As he took out a vessel to cook the rajma, Ruhi popped up from behind him, 'Are you going to let me help or not?'

'Ah! No,' Raghu said before she could reach the vessel.

Once the vessel was on the stove, he walked over to his bookshelf and began browsing through his collection. Ruhi dipped her finger into the half-cooked rajma and gave him a teasing look. She flashed him an innocent smile while slowly licking her fingers.

'What did I tell you?' he said.

'I don't know, I wasn't listening,' came the coy reply.

She took one more spoon just to tease him and let out a peal of delicious laughter. Raghu came towards her and she backed away playfully. 'You're not getting away that easily . . .' Raghu chuckled and almost caught her, his hands grazing her waist. She squealed in surprise and in her attempt to get away from him, knocked the vessel off the stove, spilling all its contents on the floor.

'Now what are we going to do? You spilled all of it.' Ruhi sighed.

Raghu giggled. 'Well, this time I'll let you make it.'

'But it's your fault, you dropped it,' she teased him, raising her eyebrows.

'Well, you were the one who distracted me with your beauty, causing me to drop it.' He had a flirty smile on.

'OK, fine.'

'How about you make more rajma while I clean up this mess?' Raghu suggested.

'Okay . . . But I don't know how it will turn out.'

'It doesn't matter, I'm sure I'll love it.'

After the second batch of rajma was cooked, they both sat down to eat, basking in each other's company. As Raghu was cleaning up the mess, Ruhi remembered the frozen chicken she had seen in the refrigerator. Unsure of whether to bring up the touchy subject, she remained quiet for a few minutes. But unable to hold herself back any longer, she finally asked, 'Raghu . . . can I ask you something?'

'Yes,' he said, throwing the wasted rajma in the bin.

'Will you take my request seriously?'

'What happened?' he asked, coming closer and holding her close.

'I want you to stop eating non-vegetarian food. Not because I'm a Brahmin , but because I personally believe that humans have no right to kill animals. Every single animal has a right to live. I know your taste buds will crave for it but do you think you could try? Just for my happiness?' Ruhi requested softly into his ears as he hugged her.

'You thought I wasn't serious about my New Year's resolution?'

'To be frank, yes.'

'That's rude.'

'No. I mean no one takes their New Year's resolutions seriously.'

'But I take you seriously. I'll throw the chicken that's in my fridge and never eat again.'

Ruhi grinned as Raghu tightened his grip on her waist. She was happier than when he had proposed; this was a commitment towards something she felt very strongly about. That night, after returning to her hostel, Ruhi slept like a baby, secure in the knowledge that Raghu respected her views and was serious about an effort to adopt them as his own.

Raghu woke up next day to an emotional message:

I never thought it would be so easy. You don't know how stressed I was by that thought. But last night, you made me feel so comfortable. I had already planned half a dozen ways to try and convince you, but not even one of them was needed. That shows how much you value this relationship and care for my feelings. I have started respecting you more, even if you did spill all the rajma on the floor. I love you. Every thought of yours is mine and every decision of mine is yours. I hope you understand the last line . . .

He smiled, and typed back, *I thought we agreed that the rajma wasn't my fault! Love you.* ☺

I love you too, Ruhi replied, followed with a dozen hearts.

'It's so good to see Raghu and Ruhi together,' Chris said, as he accompanied Megha to the lecture hall.

'Touch wood,' she replied.

'Did you consider talking to Jai again?'

'Unless I am very sure, I just can't. I like him but he has a lot to achieve in his life and I don't want to get in the way of that. I don't want to force my decision on him.'

Chris rolled his eyes. 'I'm sure you won't be forcing him.'

'I just don't want to intimidate him into making any rash decision,' Megha said, looking into her bag for her notebook. 'Oh no! I have forgotten all my notes in my room.' She rummaged through her bag once more and decided to go back to her room to get them.

'I'll move towards my lecture hall then. Hope you don't mind,' Chris said as he was already late for his lecture which was scheduled in the adjacent building.

'Sure. You carry on,' Megha replied as she walked through the corridors, taking in the beautiful landscape and pleasant sunshine, her mind drifting over happy memories. Lost in thought, she strolled along, until she glanced at her watch and realized the time. He was late.

She started walking faster and decided to take the shortcut to her room, through the back of the campus. The passage was deserted and as she walked through it, she could hear only the sound of her own footsteps. She saw a blurry figure standing at one end of the passage and something about it caught her attention; the person was standing facing the wall. As she went closer, she registered that he was urinating.

Disgusted, she shouted, 'Don't you have any etiquette? This is a college campus and you are urinating out in the open. I'll complain about you to the authorities.'

When the person turned around, she saw it was Akhilesh. And instead of apologizing, he began shouting.

'Don't teach me about rules. I am free to do as I like! Go file a complaint against me, you slut, I don't care.'

'You are such a hypocrite. Such double standards. On one hand you talk about the safety of women and their dignity and now this . . .' Megha shook her head in disgust.

'You need mental treatment. I'm not going to forget this! Mark my words, I am going to destroy you!' he shouted, staring in her direction as she started to walk away.

Megha collected her notes and went straight back to the lecture hall. She wanted to teach Akhilesh a lesson for insulting her, but she was well aware that he, as an SCI representative, had a strong network. She knew that filing a complaint against him would not do any good. Yet, she wanted to do something.

In the end, she did what she knew best—writing on Facebook.

We are creating fake revolutionaries: My open letter to the pseudo-representative of Women's Dignity, Mr Akhilesh.

I am shocked to see that a misogynist like Akhilesh is being hailed as a revolutionary. I want to ask him— Is unzipping your pants in public and urinating in the corridors part of the revolutionary tools you use to protect women's dignity?

These pseudo revolutionaries were standing up for women's safety on 31 December and stopping students from leaving the campus. Women no longer need to leave the college to feel unsafe, they can do so right here. I am writing this letter because I had an ugly encounter with this newly appointed leader Mr Akhilesh. This was not the first bad experience I have had with him, but hopefully it will be the last. He threatened me, insulted me and suggested that I need psychiatric help. When I see a male urinating in public, I feel that it is unsafe for me and my fellow females. This is what I tried to explain to him when his fragile male ego got hurt.

You claimed that you are free to do as you please, but does that mean there are no consequences for you? Is urinating in public your idea of freedom? This highlights the shallowness of your political and revolutionary ideologies. Please update your definitions of revolution and freedom. Freedom is not just about public urination and smoking in a 'No Smoking' area, it is much more than that. I am saddened and upset to see that my MGU is supporting these fake revolutionaries.

Within the next few hours, the post went viral on social media and there arose several opinions, some in favour and some against it. All her friends stood by her as she started getting harassed by Akhilesh's supporters soon after the post was uploaded. Raghu, Ruhi, Chris and Jai faced equal hostility from SCI students who tried their best to undermine them. However, they were prepared for this, knowing the unstable temperament of the SCI.

It didn't take much time for the post to be picked up by the media, and by the next day, it was breaking news throughout Delhi. Jai had asked his friends in the ABCP to keep Megha's name out of the news, as she did not want to become a political spokesperson for MGU. With the request of ABCP students, Megha's name was not mentioned anywhere.

While the SCI claimed that all the allegations in the post were false, it was the ABCP who took up the stand for women's safety and demanded that strict action be taken against Akhilesh. They firmly supported Megha and forced the authorities to take quick action. The authorities, unable to ignore such immense pressure from the students, the media and almost everyone else, reprimanded Akhilesh with a fine of Rs 5000 and a strict warning.

It was not a personal battle for Megha; she was simply fed up with the way people insulted women and did what they pleased around campus. For her, it was about promoting self-respect for every girl in the college and having the freedom to express her thoughts. She had wanted to retaliate in some form and the outcome had turned out to be better than she could ever have imagined!

Nine

27 April 2016

The mood inside the campus was uncertain. The students'
ideologies were fickle and the people who influenced
them, unreliable. While Krishna and Akhilesh left no
stone unturned to back the AISC and SCI respectively, the
ABCP too was not left far behind. The only thing on solid
ground was the friendship of Jai and his group.

Jai continued to support the ABCP whenever they needed
his help but this never distracted him from being there for his
friends in times of need. Megha too continued to voice her
opinions, no longer afraid of a retaliation from Akhilesh. She
was confident in every aspect of her life, except of her feelings
for Jai. Chris on the other hand preferred to stay away from
all the political drama on campus except when his friends

were involved. Ruhi's love affair with PETA continued and she had managed to keep Raghu away from non-vegetarian food ever since they had started dating. Raghu, on the other hand, no longer cared for non-vegetarian food since he was having the time of his life with her.

The newspapers that day, however, announced more turbulence for MGU as the story of the missing student resurfaced: *'Over 100 days and counting, MGU student Mani still missing . . . Justice delayed is justice denied . . . Protests all over but no leads found. Delhi Police fails once again in their investigations',* screamed one.

'The court hearings continue but Mani's parents feel those are just a formality as Delhi Police has lost hope with no leads after ABCP and AISC were found clean', said another

'"We have lost our kid . . . just because we are poor," claim parents of missing child', said yet another.

Mani had been missing since the first week of January and even after 100 days no one understood what exactly had happened to him. The SCI decided to term it as a big political scandal. But without any proof, their claims were baseless, especially when the Delhi Police found no involvement of the AISC or the ABCP in the matter. However, the SCI stayed strong in their stand against the AISC, who in turn continued to pass the blame to the ABCP. The slow progress of the case had put even the college administration under scrutiny.

'We will not let them overpower us. Even after strong connections have been found between the AISC and Mani's disappearance, the police have failed to take any action. A student goes missing from the national capital of India and no one knows where he is? Doesn't that make it clear that there are strong political powers involved? We must get to the truth before more steps are taken to cover up his kidnapping,' Akhilesh said, addressing his students.

When Krishna was asked about his opinion on the matter, he said that Mani might have left because he felt threatened by the ABCP. 'I don't think he has been kidnapped or been in any kind of accident. If that was the case, then the Delhi Police would have found at least one lead by now. This means that he has left of his own free will, fearing the anger of the ABCP. The case should be closed, according to me,' he said.

The ABCP stuck to what they had been saying since day one. A representative of the ABCP said, 'Haven't we been saying the same thing since the investigation began? Those who are blaming us are simply frustrated because they cannot find any concrete clues. Both the AISC and the Delhi Police have tried to pin this on us multiple times but have failed, as there is simply no evidence of our involvement. We are not looking for any political gain from this incident, all we are saying is that a student from our campus has gone missing and instead of taking any radical steps to find him, everyone is just playing blame games.'

And so the allegations continued. No one thought about the student who was probably in a dire situation, or about his parents who cried every day, fearing the worst. Every one tried to milk the situation to further their political agenda. It seemed as if the university was stuck in a raging tempest which showed no signs of abating.

✐

'I don't know why, but I feel that Jai's friends from the ABCP are behind Mani's kidnapping,' Raghu said.

'Who's Mani?' Ruhi was not in the least concerned about campus politics.

'The missing student.'

'Oh yeah, what happened about that? And why would Jai's friends do such a thing, they seemed so nice when they helped us escape campus.'

'I am not saying they are bad, I just have this gut feeling that they are somehow involved. I don't think all this business is just about the fight Mani had with the AISC and ABCP students. I think it's something bigger than that. There are many things hidden inside his missing reports which some people are trying to erase. Maybe it's because he was from another religion.'

'Raghu, you are thinking about it too much. And who talks about this stuff on a date anyway. You're supposed to be getting cosy with me, not discussing some morbid details about a student going missing,' Ruhi said, getting annoyed.

They were at Lord of the Drinks in Rajouri Garden to celebrate their three-month anniversary. Ruhi was a little upset that Raghu was lost in his own thoughts when the ambience of the restaurant was so romantic and their table so secluded. It was a perfect setting to do so many other things, rather than discuss some missing boy. When Raghu finally emerged from his thoughts, he realized that Ruhi was looking stunning. He immediately wiped away all the political drama from his head and started tickling her waist.

I'm nervous. I've never done this before. Raghu was sure he would mess it up in public.

'Don't be nervous. Mistakes are to be expected,' Ruhi said softly, sensing his anxiety. They were both a little apprehensive. After all, until now, they had kissed and explored each other only behind closed doors.

'I love the way you speak,' Raghu whispered, playing with the waistband of her skirt.

'How?'

'You are pretty outspoken in all the things that matter to you.'

'Like my love for animals?' She laughed.

'Is that your way of making me feel better?' Raghu shuddered, starting to panic about the display of public intimacy.

'What I mean is that no first time is perfect, it's not like the movies.'

'I suppose so, have you done this before?'

Damn, she must be an expert in this. I wish I had taken biology seriously or even public speaking, I would have sounded so much more confident, thought Raghu.

'It doesn't matter, you have me now. So don't be nervous,' Ruhi cajoled him.

Raghu moved closer, leaving no space between them. Reaching up to tuck her hair behind her ear, he was rewarded with a view of her bare neck. 'I really care for you, Ruhi,' he murmured.

'I care for you too, Raghu. I wouldn't want to do this with anyone else.'

'Good.'

He slid his hands down her shoulders and almost started kissing her when he heard someone say, 'Sir, your order.'

The moment Raghu realized the waiter had come to their table, he sprung away from Ruhi.

'Sir, your aloo-mattar,' the waiter said, hiding a smile.

Embarrassed, Raghu nodded but couldn't meet his eye. Ruhi adjusted her clothes as the waiter began serving them.

Raghu was shocked by her casual attitude. Seeing his alarmed face, Ruhi laughed. 'I told you, mistakes were to be expected.'

'Shit, that was so embarrassing,' he said once the waiter left, and joined in the laughter.

'The waiter did a surgical strike on us.'

'Yeah, and I was so close to kissing you.'

'I love the innocence in your eyes,' Ruhi said, shifting closer to him again.

'Why?'

'They say a lot . . . about your love for me, about your honesty in our relationship. I admire you more every day.'

'It's all you, you make me feel so comfortable, and I feel like I can finally be myself. You have transformed me, Ruhi.'

'All I did was make you realize your worth.'

After a comfortable silence, Ruhi gave him a kiss on his cheek. 'I want to change one more thing though, your susceptible nature . . .'

'Now what?'

'You were so easily convinced to make out with me in public, even though your heart was against it.'

'That's because I love you.'

'No, it's not only about me. I have seen it happen with other people too.'

'Okay, madam. Now can we eat our food or do you want to change my eating style as well?' Raghu smiled.

'Shut up.'

Raghu had always skipped the romantic parts in books, but he now understood their significance, living his own real-life romance. He even started feeling the side-effects of not attending sex education classes in school.

After finishing their dinner, they came back to a quiet campus. On the way back to Ruhi's hostel, they passed a dark and deserted stretch from the back gate. There was not a single soul to be seen, and adrenaline rushed through both of them. Ruhi glanced up to see Raghu advancing towards her.

'Are you sure?' she whispered.

'Yes, I am quite sure and this time it's not because of anyone else's influence.'

'What if someone sees us?' Ruhi said, acting coy.

'No one will come, unless you moan too loudly,' Raghu said wickedly, pinning her against the wall of the building.

He leaned down and started a trail of kisses along her neck. As she tilted her head back to give him full access, she wrapped her hands around his neck and pulled him closer. She moaned softly. She wondered how long it had been since he'd been with a girl, and shivered as his breath tickled her neck and face. His teeth skimmed the surface of her skin, not hard enough to break the surface but enough to make her weak with pleasure.

'You're such a dirty bird,' she said smirking.

'Yes, but I'm your dirty bird.'

Their eyes burned with passion and they were transported into a world of ecstasy. Raghu pushed her to the ground and began to fumble with the waistband of her skirt.

'Not here,' Ruhi interrupted.

'Are you afraid of being caught or are you getting too influenced by me?' Raghu winked, bringing up their earlier conversation of him being too easily manipulated by other people.

'None of it. But let's go to your room.'

Still in control of his senses, Raghu knew that there would be someone keeping watch over his hostel because of the missing student. He pulled Ruhi behind a bush and without wasting any time, began the art of exploration. Ruhi heard him growl in appreciation as he pulled her skirt up to her waist, seeing her body.

'You're so beautiful, Ruhi,' Raghu whispered, his voice deep with passion. 'I want to hear you scream my name. I want to hear your whimper as you beg for release.'

They looked deep into each other's eyes, disconnected from reality, lost in the wave of their emotions. Ruhi realized that every kiss before this had been wrong as he held her tightly. The bush seemed to be alight with the heat of their love.

'You are amazing. I never thought there were such intense emotions burning inside you. You can move the earth with your strength,' Ruhi said, relaxing against him,

'I can lie here with you forever. I love your voice, I love your body; I love you.' She wrapped her arms around his body, pulling him on top of her.

'We can't. Look where we are.'

'It doesn't matter, I belong to you,' she declared. Raghu let go of his past and future and surrendered himself to the moment. He was with Ruhi and she was with him, and in that second, nothing else in the world mattered.

28 April 2016

The sunbeams were reflected on Jai's teacup as he picked it up to have another sip. It was his fifth cup since the morning, which made Megha a little curious.

'Is anything wrong?'

He glanced at her, but didn't reply.

'You look lost. Is something troubling you?' she asked again.

'I'm not sure.' Jai took another sip from his cup and said, 'I don't know where to start. Maybe it's better if I keep my mouth shut.'

Burning with curiosity, Megha insisted, 'Still . . . in short, if you can.'

'It's about the missing student's case,' he finally said.

'What about it?'

'The ABCP feels that there are lots of secrets regarding the case. It's not as straight as it looks.'

'Do they have any concrete proof?' Megha asked anxiously.

'I don't know . . . I mean they have not revealed it to me yet. But they are sure Krishna is involved in something dangerous. Either Mani came to know about it or was actively involved in it—we don't know yet.'

'Mani was an active member of the SCI, right?' Megha assumed, given Akhilesh's support for him.

'No. SCI is supporting him because he's a Tamilian. Otherwise he was not an active part of any organization. But the ABCP has secretly investigated and found from his friends that he often talked about Kraanti and revolution. That's mysterious.'

'Who was he actually then?'

'Maybe just a victim.'

Lost in their own thoughts, they browsed their phones for a while, when Jai broke the silence.

'By the way, don't write any open letters on this information. Otherwise, I'll be the next person to disappear from this campus.'

'What a joke.' Megha laughed.

'Did that moron say anything to you after that?' Jai asked.

'No. He just stares and shouts rude comments whenever he sees me alone. He's the one that requires mental treatment,' Megha replied, tired of Akhilesh's antics.

'Just avoid him, if he had to do something, he would have done it by now. He doesn't have the guts.'

Megha smiled.

'But he was right about one thing,' Jai said, leaning forward on the table.

Megha looked confused. 'And what's that?'

'That you need mental treatment.' Jai burst out laughing.

'Jai!' She tried to hit him with a cup but missed, causing it to crash on the floor and break.

'See, I told you, these are the signs.'

'I am not going to forget this.' Megha ran behind him as he got up to leave the canteen.

'Do you sometimes forget that we are here to study?' Megha said with a smile as she caught up with him. They walked towards the college building.

'Yeah, with all this drama, that's the last thing on my mind. But you are doing well, aren't you?' Jai asked, referring to her high score in the previous semester.

'Not as well as you. How do you manage to balance everything in your life?'

'It's not that tough. I just stay away from all the usual addictions—girls, alcohol and smoking.'

'So you mean that people who don't fall in love don't smoke or drink? Only lovers do?'

'I am not saying that. But see, when a girl leaves a guy, he starts drinking to get over the pain which eventually leads to smoking. It's a chain effect which I don't want to risk getting into.'

'Your logic and your theories . . . keep them to yourself.' Megha was exasperated. She wanted to tell him how she felt, but his rigid beliefs made her stay quiet. She wanted to sail the oceans of love with him, but the fear of destabilizing the calm ship of their friendship held her back from taking off the mask of pretence.

Ten

22 June 2016

'Today I'm assigning you your biggest task yet. On the face of it, it may look easy but it isn't. The NGO people to whom you're supposed to be delivering the parcels today come under the high-risk bracket. That's the reason I don't want any other student to handle it except you.'

'Why is it high-risk?' asked Raghu.

'Because it's a decider. It'll decide the fate of thousands of poor Dalits and people from other lower castes; it'll decide the results of the student elections which are not far. It'll decide our fate. This time you have to bring back another bag along with you and hand over a note with the parcels. Upon arrival, you have to deliver the bags to a firm in Delhi.'

'Do you think this is the only way to fight this battle?'

Furious at being constantly questioned, Krishna reacted, 'Yes, we need to unite. They are trying to discriminate against us on religious grounds. We are only poor, not weak, and we need to be responsible citizens and stand up for what is right. If our votes count in the election, why aren't we counted as proper citizens of society? We need to provide a united front as those who truly believe in secularism, socialism and the Constitution.'

Krishna paused, then continued, 'Forget about the elections, it's about our movement and the fact that our rights are constantly being denied. It is high time we be given an equal status in society and treated with dignity, irrespective of the kind of work we do. That is the only way to fight the battle.'

Krishna's words, like always, inspired Raghu and he graciously accepted the task. He had to deliver the parcels to some part of Haryana, to a member of an NGO that helped Krishna and his team by acting as mediators. Recalling his first fearful mission, he hoped for a smooth road ahead this time. It was late in the evening and throughout the ride, he ensured that the parcels were kept well concealed. They reached Haryana within a couple of hours but the journey from there on to the location was impeded by bad roads.

After reaching Good Luck restaurant, which the drop-off point, Raghu surveyed the spot and found everything under control. He wanted to wrap up everything as soon as possible and leave, but the wait had just begun. Yet another hour passed by before Raghu checked his watch again for the umpteenth time and decided to call Krishna. But just like last time, there was no response. The restaurant as well as the hotel attached to it seemed deserted; even the receptionist was snoring. He looked at his watch again, worried by the long wait and lack of response. He wondered if he should just leave the parcels there and go, but remembered he had to collect a bag in return. Before he could decide what to do, his phone rang.

Ruhi calling.

Raghu disconnected the call and decided to open the parcels to check if it was safe to leave them there itself. As he opened the trunk of the car, he saw piles of boxes, stacked one on top of the other. He looked for a pair of scissors or a knife in the toolkit, and on finding one, began to rip open the topmost box. His phone was still ringing. Putting the box down, he picked up his phone. It was Ruhi again. Raghu took the call to ask her to stop calling when she shouted from the other end, 'I need to tell you something like right now.' She sounded worried.

'Not now, Ruhi. I will call you tonight, I am a little busy.'

'I know! But I need to tell you—'

Before she could finish, Raghu disconnected the call.

Fuck . . . how I should contact him, this is serious. Ruhi panicked when Raghu didn't pay any heed to her requests. She needed to get in touch with him somehow, to tell him what she had heard, or rather, what she was still listening to, standing outside a classroom. She heard hushed voices,

'Just a little more time and Raghu will be the next one.'

'You mean . . . are you serious, even after so much of chaos?'

'It's not me who has decided that. Also, he's not going to be facing it alone.'

'Then?'

'Both of them,' the voice confirmed.

Ruhi's mind spun at what she had overheard. She tried to peep into the classroom, to see who was talking. One thing was clear—the second voice belonged to Krishna. She had even seen him go inside. Ruhi was sure he was involved in something illegal, but no matter how many times she called Raghu, he kept disconnecting her call. Scared of being seen by the students inside, she left the corridor, knowing she had to do something to help Raghu. His life was in danger.

Raghu cut open one of the boxes and couldn't believe his eyes. In a second, all his beliefs crashed. His life's goals and ambitions came to a screeching halt as he ripped open

a few more boxes. With every box, he grew angrier, as he realized that he was just a puppet controlled by Krishna. The revolution and Kraanti were all just an act to provoke him into conducting their illicit affairs. They were not helping the poor or the people from lower castes. He had been manipulated by people who were propagating fake ideologies. Raghu was suddenly aware that this scandal was much bigger than Krishna; there were bigger political parties pulling the strings and even the NGOs were involved.

Every box that Raghu had brought along had bundles of notes. The car was filled with money. Raghu had no idea where the money came from, but he understood that it was put in the names of NGOs to keep it hidden. Remembering the note he had been instructed to deliver, he tore open the envelope as well and read the message.

Hope the material this time is of better quality and not like last time when we targeted the DLF Mall area near MGU for the riots. Your money is safe in the boxes.

Raghu went numb. That was the same incident that had caused a fight with his friends and almost cost him the love of his life. It changed his outlook towards everything, and even if indirectly, he had been supporting the people responsible for it all along. Raghu was overcome with fear and froze at the spot. Suddenly he felt his phone vibrate; it was Krishna. *Wait at the location itself. A car will be reaching the spot soon. Be alert and safe.*

He looked around to see if anyone was watching him. Every time he glanced around, he felt a pair of eyes following his every move. He had a million questions and his head hurt with confusion; the person who was advising him to be safe was the one who had put him in this dangerous situation. But worse was his guilt. The note was the clue, and all the pieces fit now.

It was all his fault. He was the one to blame for arguing with his friends, for being so easily manipulated and, most importantly, for putting Ruhi's life in danger. All this time he had been helping the people who had initiated the incident that almost took Ruhi away from him, forever.

Eleven

28 April 2016

Ruhi was still in the fortress of her bed, cocooned in her blanket, when her phone buzzed. She had been thinking about the previous night and wanted to lose herself once more in the memories of her and Raghu together. She reached over and smiled as she read Raghu's message.

While there are many things I am unsure of, you are not one of them. You're the only girl for me. I always knew our friendship would blossom into something bigger. You are the warmth I need to keep me safe in this dark world. Before you came into my life I was just an average guy in an average world, there was always something missing. Today, I realized exactly what I was missing, it was you. Everything about you, from the way you act, to the way you love me, makes me believe that I will never get tired of you. You were a rock star last night and revealed parts of me I didn't even know existed until we made love. For this, I will forever be grateful and look forward to the life we will share. There are some things in life beyond our control. The sun will rise and set, the tide will continue to flow, the seasons will continue to change and I will continue to love you.

Unable to resist herself, Ruhi replied in a second:

You know, while thinking about last night, I discovered there is something mysterious about our relationship. This relationship is almost a thing in itself and yet it is something no one can see or touch. I share so much with you and have told you things I never imagined telling anyone. It is you I want to wake up next to, you who I want to grow old with. I am the same person I have always been and yet the friendship I discovered with you has shown me new dimensions of life I could never have imagined. I understand this love we share may pose a difficulty in the future, but I am perfectly fine with that. There'll be tough times, but there will be a hundred more happy ones. I love you.

I love you too. Let's go out somewhere, came Raghu's reply.

Not now. I need to attend my history class. You know Professor Nair is very strict. After the lecture then?

Done.

🎤

'We did it yesterday,' Ruhi said, blushing.

'Are you serious?' Megha threw her a surprised look. 'Where?'

'Campus.'

'Wow, that's unreal. You are crazy.'

Megha wanted to know every detail and Ruhi didn't spare any. She gave a minute-to-minute narration of the incident. The only person who had an objection to this heated discussion was Mrs Nair, their history teacher, who warned them about gossiping in class. However, unable to contain her excitement, Megha continued to discuss further. A little later in the lecture, she took a deep breath, feeling uneasy. Ruhi made her drink some water but the uneasiness abided in her.

'Ma'am, I am unable to sit and concentrate. I have a recurring migraine problem and my head is hurting very badly.'

'So what do you want me to do? To stop this class just because you can't concentrate. You didn't seem very interested to begin with,' Professor Nair said bluntly.

'Can I skip the class please? I am unable to focus, everything is blurry,' she said slowly.

'Okay, you can leave. Ruhi, you can go along and help her.'

'Yes, ma'am.' Ruhi was happy to oblige.

'Ma'am, my attendance?' Megha asked, not wanting to lose out on the first twenty minutes she had spent in the class.

'You just skip the class and take care.'

Professor Nair turned back and began addressing the rest of the students. Though happy that they could leave, the girls were still unsure about their attendance. But they knew that Professor Nair was very strict and normally never changed her mind. So they left, with the professor's eyes following them till they stepped out of the classroom.

'Are you okay?' Ruhi asked, holding her hand.

'My headaches come quite frequently these days. I'll have to tell the doctor to change my medicines.'

'Do you think Mrs Nair will mark our attendance?'

'Ideally, she should, but you never know with her,' Megha said. 'Now finish your story.'

Ruhi laughed and continued telling her tale. When she was done, Megha decided to go rest in her room for a while, while Ruhi messaged Raghu.

He had been waiting for her message, and they decided to go to DLF Mall.

'I feel so inferior when I come to shopping malls like these and see the amount of money people spend,' Raghu commented as they walked towards the food court.

'Don't feel bad. Even these people are constantly looking for sales and offers to make things cheaper. Otherwise even they buy everything online at a cheaper rate.' Ruhi laughed.

'Will you feel bad if I don't buy you clothes from H&M or a fancy bag from Zara?'

'Don't be a fool, Raghu. If that was what I wanted from a relationship, I had a million other options. I'm with you because I love you, and not your money. I won't mind even if you buy me clothes from Sarojini,' she joked.

They both smiled at each other and after a little while, found an empty table. Raghu glanced at the options and asked, 'What'll you have?'

'I am not really hungry. You want to have something?' Ruhi asked him, scanning the numerous choices in front of her.

'Don't worry; I can afford a pizza.' Raghu grinned.

Ruhi agreed and watched him as he went to order a pizza and juice for both of them. While standing at the counter, she saw him opening his bag and putting a small box inside his pocket. When he walked back to the table she caught him red-handed.

'What are you hiding?'

'Nothing,' Raghu said, avoiding the question and looking everywhere but at her face.

'Come on, I saw you putting something into your pocket while you were standing at the counter.'

'That's not fair.'

'Please?' said Ruhi, guessing it was something for her. Raghu told her to close her eyes while he took the small box out of his pocket. Sitting with her chin resting on her hands, Ruhi almost lost her balance when Raghu pulled one of her hands and placed the box in it. She smiled widely in anticipation.

'This is for you, to symbolize our love. I know that when I tell you that you are the most beautiful woman I have ever seen, it sounds like pure flattery, but it is true. You are the epitome of everything I have ever wished for. And although this is not twenty-four-carat gold, it carries my twenty-four-carat love.'

Ruhi opened her eyes and saw Raghu holding a ring in his hand. He slowly slipped it on her finger and kissed her hand. Blushing, Ruhi got up from her chair and went around the table to give him a kiss on his cheek. Raghu got a little uncomfortable with all the eyes on them. But Ruhi didn't care. Despite his limited means, this guy had tried to gift her the perfect gift, just to show what she meant to him, and it touched the core of her heart.

As they made their way back, Ruhi and Raghu were suddenly surrounded by a nervous crowd—people were in a state of panic, screaming and running helter-skelter. Some men had pulled up in big cars and trucks, brandishing powerful weapons. They were randomly and brutally lashing out at everyone they could get hold of while shouting slogans against the lower castes.

Terrified, Raghu grabbed Ruhi's hand and began to run. They ran past broken shops, scenes of crying children and a cloud of wails. Dust rose as people scrambled to get away. Amid all the chaos, Ruhi tripped and fell, landing on her jaw. Raghu bent down to help her when he felt a hard blow on his back. His whole body exploded with pain as he realized that he had been hit with an iron rod. The merciless blows came again and again, even as Ruhi howled and screamed. Somehow Raghu managed to brave the pain and push off his attacker. Pulling Ruhi along he shouted, 'Run!' The riots continued and the air was thick with the cries of people. Tears streamed down Ruhi's face as Raghu turned into a narrow, isolated lane. 'I can't walk any more,' she said, stumbling.

Looking back to see if anyone from the mob had tried to follow them, Raghu made her sit on the edge of the road and went to look for water. Except for a few children, the road was deserted. Scared to be left alone, Ruhi shouted after him, 'Raghu . . . Raghu . . .'

'Okay, let's leave.' He came back and gently helped her up.

Raghu looked at Ruhi helplessly as they walked towards the university. He couldn't believe what had just happened; the slogan-shouting, the mob and specially the way that man had looked at him while hitting him. Like Raghu didn't deserve to live. They had had nothing to do with the riots, but had been targeted nonetheless. And he had been unable to protect Ruhi.

Before they entered the campus, Raghu made her sit outside at a dhaba and wiped the blood from her chin. He handed her a glass of water while he went to wash his face. Ruhi remained silent throughout, not uttering a single word even when they took the turn towards her hostel. Raghu stopped her and turned her towards him. 'Are you feeling better now?' he asked softly.

Though her physical injuries weren't serious, the mental trauma she had endured was too much for her to handle. Sensing her misery, Raghu wrapped his arms around her and pulled her close. Finally feeling safe, Ruhi broke down. 'I thought I lost you . . . that I would lose my own life . . . I thought I would never meet my parents again . . .' she wept.

'Don't worry, baby, I am safe now. I won't let anything happen to you. We are both safe and that's what matters the most,' Raghu said, ignoring his own fierce pain in order to comfort her.

'I'm too scared to leave the campus again. I just want to be with you . . .' Ruhi said haltingly.

'Yes, I will stay with you, always. Now calm down, everything will be all right.' Raghu continued to comfort her although he knew it would take a while before she felt safe again. He dropped her off at the girls' hostel and walked away, completely shaken.

As he walked back to his room, Raghu felt ashamed of his position in society, ashamed that his freedom was constantly taken away from him although he harmed no one and only tried to find happiness with the ones he loved. What hurt him the most though was that Ruhi could end up being made to suffer because of the accident of his birth.

Twelve

29 April 2016

'Is Ruhi all right?' Chris asked.

He and Raghu were returning from a walk. Still traumatized by the incident, Raghu needed to clear his head.

'I tried to comfort her, that's all I can do right now,' he said. 'What scared me most was not the fear of death, but the fear of their hatred. Their terrible slogans and the violence against people like me made me question a lot of my beliefs.'

'It's not like that, this wasn't a personal attack on you. You just happened to be in the wrong place at the wrong time. There were many others too.'

'There they are.' It was Akhilesh, pointing at Raghu and Chris walking down the road towards the campus.

'But Megha isn't even with them, neither is Jai,' replied one of his friends.

'It doesn't matter; they all belong to the same group. The whole lot of them deserve to be taught a lesson.'

'Are you sure?'

'Yes, just let them come closer, and then we will attack,' Akhilesh declared.

Akhilesh was still furious at the fine that had been imposed on him because of Megha's Facebook post. Nursing a grudge since that day, he was determined to show the whole group what happened when they mess with the leader of the SCI. This was the perfect opportunity: the issue had cooled down and her group was emotionally scattered by the riots. Surveying the area to make sure there were no cops around, he gave his group the signal to attack.

'That's the problem. Religion is something personal for me, not something that I publicize; that's why even this mass attack feels personal,' Raghu said.

'Hmm.' Chris nodded.

'They wanted to stop us from socializing; stop all the people of lower castes. How ridiculous is that? What if something had happened to her? Who would have been responsible?' he went on.

'But nothing serious happened, right?'

'Yes, today nothing serious happened, but can you say the same about tomorrow?'

'You are just overthinking this; it was a one-off thing. Don't take it so personally.'

'But it was personal! They attacked Ruhi because she was with me, just because she was with someone from a lower caste. There were others there too. Why weren't they targeted?'

'Think logically, Raghu. How would they know which caste you are from? They just targeted people randomly, their motive was violence,' Chris tried to reason.

'I am thinking logically and that's why I feel unsafe now . . . I just can't get over the attack.'

And just as he had said that, Akhilesh's gang fell upon them. They beat them with sticks, chains—whatever they could get their hands on.

'Let us go, you bastards!' Raghu shouted.

He couldn't see the faces of his attackers since they had all worn masks. One of the goons caught hold of Raghu by the shoulder and threw him to the ground. Another tried to stab Chris, while Akhilesh began kicking Raghu in the stomach. Despite being outnumbered, Chris managed to free himself from the boy who held on to him and ran to help Raghu, who was then being strangled by Akhilesh.

'Let him go, you son of a bitch!' Chris yelled, trying to punch him. Before long, a crowd gathered around them, causing the SCI members to disperse. But before leaving, Akhilesh pulled off his mask to reveal his identity.

'You all deserve this. Remember never to mess with us again, because next time it will be much worse,' he spat out and walked away briskly, leaving Raghu and Chris lying on the road, bleeding and badly hurt. No one in the crowd came up to help them; instead, some spectators pulled out their phones and began recording the scene. Both the boys tried to hide their faces in shame; they had never experienced anything like this before. Attacked the second time in such a short spell, Raghu felt exhausted—both physically and mentally. He was bruised and scratched, but the greatest damage had been to his soul. Disillusioned with society, he seriously began to fear for his life.

'You should file a complaint. How do they think they can get away with something like this?' Megha almost shouted, furious when she found out about the incident.

Raghu was too traumatized to speak and despite the best efforts of his friends to comfort him, remained quiet.

'Please say something,' Ruhi pleaded, forgetting about her own breakdown just a few hours earlier. 'I don't know what to say . . .'

'Someone has to stop these people,' Jai finally said.

Chris too was in shock but slowly regained his composure. 'I think Akhilesh just wanted to show his superiority after Megha humiliated him publicly,' he said.

'Then why did they attack us? Are you still claiming this wasn't personal, that they targeted us randomly?' This time it was Raghu breaking his silence.

Chris had no answer to that.

Raghu looked at him and continued, 'If it was just about Megha, he would have done this long ago. Why did he wait for such a long time and even then target only us?'

'Raghu, calm down. We are there for you, *I'm* here for you,' Ruhi tried to pacify him.

'No, you are not there for me. There is no one who can support me or the people of my community. We are not the elite class, we are just the backward class who have no right to live in this society full of hypocrites.'

'Raghu, what's wrong with you? We are your friends; we will always be there for you. Please calm down.' Ruhi was surprised at his reaction.

'No, Ruhi, I can't calm down. You were there with me, and you got attacked; what was your fault in being with me? Just because you were with me, you suffered. I can't calm down,' he said and threw his phone down in anger. 'They think we are weak, but I won't let this happen again.' And just like that, shutting himself from the pleading and shouting voices of his friends, Raghu stormed out of the room. His world had been shaken, his thoughts, beliefs, his entire outlook towards life put into question. And this change didn't happen gradually, it happened in the blink of an eye.

30 April 2016

Alone and depressed, Raghu wandered around the campus with a variety of thoughts running through his head. He had thought he had the freedom to do as he liked, to go where he pleased; but that was not the case. The events of the day forced him to accept he could never live freely—all because he was from a lower caste. He couldn't wrap his head around the fact that people like him were denied such basic rights, every day.

I feel trapped, trapped in a box that I can't get out of. No matter how hard I try, I will always belong to the same caste. It doesn't matter that I am screaming at the top of my lungs, no one can hear me in this box. I feel like I'm running out of air, running out of time, while the walls of the box continue to cave in on me. The more I try to escape, the smaller it becomes. I want to feel alive; I want to live a free and happy life with nothing holding me back. But I can't, because I'm trapped, trapped in my caste and trapped in this college.

'I can help you, you'll be safe with us,' a voice pulled him out of his thoughts.

Looking up, Raghu saw Krishna standing in front of him. 'I came to know what happened, and as a leader of the AISC, I stand by you. Those people want to make you feel like you have no place in society, but we are here to break those boundaries and question everything the caste system has to say. The AISC stands by you,' he said.

'But why? I have nothing to do with all this.' Raghu was confused.

'We all need to unite. The SCI and the ABCP are trying to undermine and destroy us, but that is happening in all the universities across India because they fear the potential in us. You say you have nothing to do with all this, but they won't let you live your life. They are denying our right to speak out against caste discrimination. We have to stop this wave of intolerance.'

Raghu was not fully convinced, but the events of the day kept playing in his mind. He was a victim of caste discrimination and Krishna used that knowledge to make the most of the situation and get him to join their movement. Raghu was dimly aware of this manipulation, but his anger overshadowed that thought, and he agreed to meet other students who had experienced similar discrimination.

'Even I am from a lower caste. The SCI almost ruined my career by spreading malicious rumours about me in public . . .' Raghu heard one of the students say at the meet.

'The ABCP thinks only they understand what nationalism is. They simply condemn everyone else,' said another.

Every person around him urged Raghu to become a part of the AISC. Overwhelmed by the mountain of information before him, he found the boundaries between right and wrong blurring. He had a tough decision to take.

The discussion continued. Krishna, noticing Raghu's hesitation, decided to dig the knife deeper. 'You are friends with Jai, who secretly supports the ABCP. Did you ever wonder why it was only you and Chris who were attacked, and not him?'

Raghu moved a little. Krishna continued, 'They didn't even do anything to Megha, even though she was the one who wrote the post. It's because you are from a lower caste and they feel they can do anything to you. You say you love Ruhi, but she told you to stop eating chicken . . .'

'How do you know that?' Raghu suddenly demanded.

'That doesn't matter here. The point is, she told you to stop eating chicken and you agreed. It's because her religion does not allow it and neither do her parents. But who are they to decide what we can and cannot eat? Did we ever tell them to stop eating potato? Why are we the only ones who have to change?'

The brainwashing continued, until Raghu's head hurt. He had no idea what to do and whom to believe. He had avoided meeting anyone, including Ruhi, that day but Krishna convinced him to attend another of their meetings after college hours and then make his decision. It was in this meeting that Raghu heard a professor, Mrs Nair, criticize Hinduism for its violence and brutality.

'Hindu society must be one of the most brutal societies in the world; it is deep-rooted in violence,' Mrs Nair said, addressing the students on the topic of politics.

'Isn't Hinduism all about peace? To suppress the devil inside and become more righteous? It was never about violence. You as a professor of MGU should pass on the correct information rather than fabricating stories,' Raghu interjected.

It was at that moment when Krishna took over and led him to believe that they were not against any religion, but against those organizations which wanted to impose their beliefs on the lower castes. By the end of it, Raghu was convinced that he was a victim of a religious war, and that the only way to rebel against it was by joining his movement. Krishna explained the work that they did and how Raghu could help them.

'See, our organization is for the youth of our community. Youth like you who have suffered. The motive of our movement is to spread the correct virtues of humanity and to help people educate themselves about basic human rights. We have a core section in the AISC, where the more dedicated students are given important tasks to execute. Teachers come from different universities to guide us in the right direction. I want you to join us. You just need to work on weekends. Would you like to join that team and spread our cause?'

Proud to be given a task of such great importance, Raghu not only joined the team but also took charge of the delivery of books and stationery to Ambala the next morning, which was generally assigned to dedicated students. Krishna promised to promote him once the task was completed successfully. Raghu did not tell his friends anything about his involvement in Kraanti, the movement. He didn't even tell Ruhi. All he said was that he had a family emergency and would be back the same night. What he didn't realize was that to solve one problem, he had set himself up for a hundred more.

Once the task of delivering the parcels had been successfully completed, Raghu received a message from Krishna: *Good Job. My man said he received the boxes in perfect condition. You are now officially a part of 'Kraanti'.*

Thirteen

27 May 2016

'Good morning,' Raghu greeted Ruhi who was glued to the screen of her mobile phone. They were at the campus café—their regular hang-out.

'Hi!' Ruhi replied, looking up momentarily before going back to staring at her phone.

'Coffee?' he asked, flipping through the menu.

'No,' she replied nonchalantly.

Raghu picked up the newspaper lying on the table and began reading out the front-page headlines aloud. His eyes went to the top right-hand corner of the paper, where the date was printed. How time had flown! A lot had changed since that fateful day of the attacks, yet the memories remained fresh. And just as painful. Over time, Raghu had retreated into a shell. He wouldn't talk as much and would remain reserved, even with Ruhi. He still loved her but the guilt that her life was put in jeopardy because of him still burdened him. Ruhi, on the contrary, had completely moved on from the incident and never once blamed Raghu for what had happened.

'Your coffee,' the waiter announced, placing the cup on the table in front of him.

'Can you get her a Coke, please? She is too busy reading my *kundali* to predict the future and doesn't have time to order,' Raghu said in mock seriousness.

'Raghu, stop it! I'm reading something important related to academics.'

'Okay, please continue,' he replied, flipping through the paper.

Raghu's change in behaviour had created an air of awkwardness among his friends. Although Jai, Chris and Megha had made peace with his behaviour over time, there was a bit of hesitancy when they interacted with him. Raghu had never been the outspoken kind, but he had become quieter after the incident. He continued working for Kraanti, and with each meeting, his way of thinking, his ideology underwent a massive change. Krishna's company and nudges from other AISC members converted him completely. So despite pretending otherwise, the dynamics of friendship in his group changed.

'What's up, people?' Megha entered the café and pulled out a chair for herself.

Raghu continued to read the newspaper while Ruhi mumbled a feeble 'hi'.

'You guys look a little off today. Especially you, Raghu. Anything serious?' Megha asked with concern.

'No,' Raghu answered uninterestedly.

Everyone in their circle had realized that Raghu was going to take time to get over the incident, so they thought it best to give him space. However, no one knew that the seeds of the wrong ideology had already been sown within his mind and day by day, Krishna was watering it until it would become a full-grown tree. They would meet once or twice a week, at odd hours— either for the AISC meeting or for some tasks related to Kraanti. Gradually, Raghu became an active participant in the meetings and would express his views more openly than before.

The only time he felt something was amiss was when he was either assigned the task of delivering parcels or asked to monitor those sent by others. He was never told the what, when and where of the task, and since he was a new member, he didn't probe either for fear of offending the higher-ups. 'Ruhi, I wanted to speak to you about something,' Raghu suddenly broke the air of nonchalance.

'Just hold on, one second. I'm almost done reading,' Ruhi replied scrolling down on her phone. Raghu was deep in thought even as Megha observed him in silence.

'I thought . . .'

'Okay, so sorry, sweetheart. What do you want to say, baba?' Ruhi asked, pulling his cheeks.

'I don't know how to tell you this but I think I will have to now. I . . . I have been hiding something from you,' Raghu said, sounding a little nervous.

'What is it?' Ruhi asked, casting a glance at Megha.

'You want me to go?' Megha asked, thinking they might want to talk in private.

'No, it's OK. You're no stranger,' Ruhi immediately replied.

'Okay, I'm going to come straight to the point. I have been meeting Krishna these past few days and have also attended a few AISC meetings post the attack. What they propagate makes a lot of sense to me and I think I subscribe to their ideology.'

'What? You've been meeting them? What's the need for it?' Ruhi asked in alarm.

'You're asking about the need? Really? Haven't you faced the music?' Raghu questioned back.

Sensing things were heating up, Megha got up from her chair to leave.

'Megha, wait!' Ruhi tried to stop her friend but she was already gone by then.

Turning back at Raghu, she nearly screamed, 'What's wrong with you?!'

An awkward silence filled the air. Both Raghu and Ruhi stared at each other for a few moments before he finally came clean on how it all started. Ruhi was not sure if Krishna could be trusted; she had got a lot of negative feedback on him from Jai and the others. Even then she wanted to hear Raghu's side of the story.

After patiently hearing him out, she didn't say anything immediately. 'I'll love you . . . but only as long as you are right,' she finally said. 'The day I find you embroiled in something you shouldn't be a part of, I will not stand by you. I love you but not over my dignity. I still don't believe that Krishna is the right person to be hanging out with. But since you seem so sure, I won't stop you. I don't want to be a nagging girlfriend who tells her partner what he should or shouldn't do.'

'Don't worry, I won't do anything wrong. I know my friends will hesitate to support me, but maybe one day I'll make them see what I see. I'll make them believe. And with your support, I will one day.'

'I love you,' Ruhi said, giving him a peck on the cheek. Her smile was enough to make him believe she meant it.

As they made their way back towards their class, they saw Jai, Megha and Chris marching furiously towards them.

'Are you serious about supporting Krishna?' Jai asked Raghu harshly.

Raghu nodded in the affirmative.

'May I know the reason?'

Silence.

'You do know that he is involved in a lot of wrongdoings, right?' Jai asked again.

'Who are you to decide what's wrong and right?' Raghu said sharply.

'Your friend who cares for you, who treats you like a brother. So stop acting like a fool and stop letting them brainwash you. Why do you want to get into the politics of casteism anyway? Stay away. We are here to study and study alone, okay?'

Ruhi became uncomfortable with the way the argument was advancing. Harsh words were exchanged and Raghu kept throwing random accusations at everyone. Soon, a small crowd of students gathered around to watch the drama. 'Enough, everyone!' Raghu screamed. 'We've been considered fools for far too long, but not any more. Yes, I belong to the lower caste but that doesn't make me any less human. Anyway, there's no going back from here as I have made up my mind. I am not saying this is wrong and that is right, but for me, saffronization is wrong.'

Raghu's fired-up attitude and his words convinced his friends that he had been far too brainwashed to understand their reasoning.

He continued, 'Chris, it's better if you realize what is happening soon. Otherwise you will be termed as an adarsh liberal by these bhakts and they will snatch your identity. Instead of arguing with me, you should ask him what he thinks about our existence.'

'Dude, for me, my friends are much more important than all this fucking drama. I don't care about caste, religion and all that bullshit. All I know is we are friends and things are getting really weird. Get out of all this bullshit while there's still time. You think by doing all this, you will become a hero? All you will do is lose track of your career. Don't let that happen,' Chris pleaded. 'Ruhi, drill some sense into your guy.'

'Don't bring Ruhi into this,' Raghu warned. Ruhi stood rooted in a corner, watching them silently.

'You're going too far, Raghu,' Jai said in a tone that was threatening and yet concerned. 'We're all friends here. Calm down and think about what you are accusing me of. What has gotten into you, Raghu? You don't even sound like yourself. This is not you talking! I'm sure someone else has put these words into your mouth. Remember I told you once that anyone can manipulate you? You better get some psychiatric help before you lose your marbles completely.'

'Do you think I have no opinions of my own? Do you think I can't stand up for my own rights? I will show you!' Seething with anger, Raghu lifted his hand to punch Jai but Chris intervened and pushed him aside. A relationship that was nurtured over so much time, now stood on the brink of complete breakdown in just a few minutes.

'Fuck off!' Jai screamed in anger.

'You fuck off, dickhead!' Raghu shot back.

Jai couldn't take the insults any more and decided to leave. He had treated Raghu like a brother but what did he get in return? Nothing, except for baseless allegations. Nothing meant more to him than their friendship, which seemed to now be sinking faster and deeper than the *Titanic*.

28 May 2016

'Comrades, we need to understand that this election is happening at a time when there are continuous efforts being made to disrupt the communal environment in colleges. We just cannot run away by blaming the ABCP. After the attacks on students like Raghu, people have been talking about putting up a united front, but AISC has been talking about unity since the very beginning.' Krishna was addressing a group of students in a classroom. They had all gathered for their weekly AISC meeting. Among them was Raghu, listening to Krishna's speech in rapt attention.

'Don't you think AISC and SCI should have jointly fought the election?' a student asked. 'Since both parties are fighting for the rights of the lower caste, their ideology would not be very different from each other. Together we could be stronger.'

'We did try to. When we proposed to the SCI that we should fight the upcoming elections together to rule out the ABCP, they said that our unity would have been more against the idea of the SCI itself, rather than for the cause of the lower caste or minority groups. I don't think we would have been able to convince them otherwise. We need to focus on our activities alone and put up a united front so we can seek a mandate for our policies.'

University elections were scheduled in the coming months and preparations were in full swing. Krishna and his troops discussed their plan of action till the wee hours of the morning. Raghu was an active participant in these talks and would listen to every topic that was raised, offering his own suggestions when called for. At the same time, he was equally hurt that his friends did not stand by him when he needed them the most. He tried to put up a brave front but every now and then he would get flashes of the good times they spent together and would wish to relive them.

'Raghu, you need to start work on the ground now. Elections are round the corner and we need to have our word out in order to start garnering support for our party,' Krishna stated.

'What am I supposed to do?' he asked.

'Just be with us during campaigning. We'll tell you the specifics as we go along.' Krishna smiled.

'Okay,' Raghu agreed.

For a moment, he thought of going back to Jai and apologizing, but his ego wouldn't let him. He spoke to Ruhi about his conflicting thoughts and she consoled him saying everything would be back to normal in no time. But her words sounded hollow.

'We are not afraid of ABCP, we are afraid of AISC,' Akhilesh confided to his team.

'And why do you think that? The students will support us too,' one of his teammates replied.

'Of course, they will. But we don't have the shrewdness like them. We stay within the four walls of the campus and concentrate on our careers too. But a person like Krishna wants to spread negativity throughout the nation. A person who can separate the best of friends and make them fight against each other can go to any extent to prove his supremacy. He is using Raghu as a tool for the upcoming elections.'

Krishna's dirty game of manipulation was evident even to Akhilesh. But the victim, Raghu, went as he was pulled along, a mere puppet in somebody else's hands.

Where not only friends but even students like Akhilesh could figure out why Krishna wanted Raghu's support, unfortunately, it was only Raghu who was blind to Krishna's true nature. The clash of egos had ruined the best of relationships.

&

'Don't you think he is going astray? Why don't you talk to him about it . . . make him understand that what he's doing is wrong?' Megha asked Ruhi as they sat in one of the empty classrooms in the lecture building.

'He has requested me to give him some time. To prove that he is right. I just don't want to force my decision on him right now. Only time will decide who is right and who is wrong. But I've told Raghu that if I ever find out that what he is doing is wrong, I will end our relationship that very moment.'

'But we were . . .'

'Nothing's going to change between us! I am your friend and I'll always be. I promise you that if he ever does something unethical, you'll be the first person I'll confide in. Still, if you insist, I'll talk to him once.'

Megha gave a weak smile; her efforts at making things the way they were among the friends were not proving to be very fruitful.

A few minutes later, Jai and Chris joined the girls.

'Do you know what Raghu's been up to? He is supporting Krishna in the upcoming elections,' Megha said looking at Jai.

'I know,' he replied with a look of disdain. 'Didn't I tell you Raghu can be easily brainwashed? Right now, Krishna has taken full control of his mental faculties; it's nearly impossible to show Raghu right from wrong. We need to prove to him that he is being misled by a bunch of bogus people who are nothing but liars and fabricators.'

'We just can't let him ruin his life like this,' Megha said, the desperation evident in her voice. 'To be with students like Krishna is like digging your own grave.'

'We cannot let him go. We need to bring him back on the right track,' Chris added.

'But how?'

'By manipulating him again, this time for the right reasons,' Jai said, turning towards Megha. 'Megha, you'll stand for the elections. You'll be a presidential candidate this year. I'll have a chat with ABCP about it.'

'*Have you gone nuts?* I don't want to get involved in this.'

'I don't want you to but we have to, for Raghu's sake. We owe him this as friends. I am sure they will try their best to win this election—by hook or by crook—but we will be righteous. And when Raghu sees the difference, he will come back to us. That's my word. I know him in and out, trust me on this. We cannot make him understand with words and if we don't do this now, we will lose him forever.'

'But why me? You're more suitable for this job.'

'No, people know you more than they know me.'

'Oh please! You're involved in so much social work along with the ABCP. Students know it and appreciate it. At least your language department does.'

'Only my department can't help us win. Students from all departments, including your own, know you because of your stand against Akhilesh. Your open letter was as viral in our university as *Ab ki baar, Modi sarkar* in the country,' Jai said with a wide smile.

'I still don't understand how you can make this work,' Ruhi intervened in a frustrated tone.

'Ruhi, you believe me, right? Then just do one thing for us. Back him up. Don't make him feel like you're with us—on our side. It's just a matter of time before things get back to normal, I promise.'

'I was thinking of talking to him once more,' Ruhi said.

'Go ahead. But I don't think talking will work at this stage. I see this as the only way out,' Jai concluded.

Later in the day, Jai had a word with his friends at ABCP and after a few rounds of discussions with the senior representatives at the party, they were convinced that Megha was the right candidate for the president's post. Not only was she dynamic, she also had the guts to take a stand against injustice and had proved it on more than one occasion.

Their only condition was this: Jai had to be the covering candidate. If, on technical grounds of anomaly in filing nomination papers, the main candidate's papers are rejected, the covering candidate becomes the official party candidate.

With no option, Jai agreed to fill the forms himself even though he couldn't understand the logic behind it. All he could see was a vision of Megha standing as the candidate and that made him happy. The plan to bring Raghu back to his senses had been set in motion.

In the next couple of days, the required forms were filled up and the respective student wings announced their support for Krishna, Akhilesh and Megha.

Fourteen

11 June 2016

'To be frank, Raghu, I don't like how you've been behaving with people around you these past couple of weeks,' Ruhi complained. They were sitting in an empty classroom and Ruhi decided it was the perfect moment for a confrontation.

'What do you mean? Have I changed?' Raghu asked.

'Ask yourself. You were never like this. You have gone against Jai, Chris—everyone.'

'Not you.'

'Does it matter?'

'It does. At least to me.'

'If it did, then you wouldn't have cut yourself off from your friends. Why is it so difficult for you to understand that they want the best for you?'

'You're under the wrong impression. They don't want to have anything to do with me. They couldn't care less about me, frankly. And I'm always made to feel like I'm in the wrong. This time, I'll prove that I am correct and Jai is wrong for a change,' Raghu said in a high-pitched voice.

'Why don't you clear these conflicts personally with him? You feel everyone is wrong but you?' Ruhi kept her calm; she didn't want to let go of this opportunity.

'I have no issues clearing things out personally with them, but what I can't fathom is if I am standing with the right people and fighting for our rights, then why can't they be okay with it? Why can't they support me in my decision? If, for once, I'm taking a stand in my life, it doesn't mean that I want to end everything else among all of us. It's they who decided to stand for the election. I didn't take that decision.'

'It's all for you,' Ruhi insisted, not ready to give up.

But Raghu was in no mood to relent. 'Let me make things clear since I don't think you're getting it—nothing is being done for me. Everyone has their own personal agenda for everything, and I'm pretty certain there must be one behind this too. That's the only reason he has decided to stand against me . . . once again. And why are you acting like his lawyer and defending him?'

That did it—Ruhi finally lost her cool.

'Wow, just wow. I fucking try to sort things out and you end up insulting me and calling me his lawyer? If you think it's all my fault, then I'll stay away from all this. Even you.' She stormed out of the classroom without another word.

Realizing he had taken it too far, Raghu got up and tried hard to stop her, but seeing the rage in her eyes, he let her go. He didn't want to create any more complications; she was the only emotional support he had now—the one who stood by him through thick and thin. After she disappeared from sight, Raghu sat down in silence for a few minutes. Then he dialled her number on an impulse but she cut the call. He tried a few more times—each time she disconnected it. Eventually, he left her a message,

I'm so sorry, I didn't mean to come off as rude. I need all your support at this time. I am not doing anything which would hurt you or shame you for being with me. Try to understand me for once and give me time to prove myself. I think I deserve at least a little time, don't I? You know how much I love you, adore you and respect you. Remember that one time when you laughed so hard while drinking a glass of chocolate milk that some of it came oozing out of your nose? I fell in love with you right then! I've been in a terrible state of mind these past few months, but every time I see you, my problems disappear. Be with me, Ruhi. I need you.

Suddenly, Raghu felt all alone in his fight to prove himself. And without Ruhi by his side, everything seemed worthless.

As he sat there staring at his mobile screen, he thought to himself, *I don't know what lies ahead but I want everyone to give me one last chance. How do I make my friends understand that Krishna is genuinely fighting for the rights of the poor? I know my friends are genuine and I know they care for me, but can't I have a different opinion? And is it wrong to stand for what I believe is right? My intentions are not wrong but my fault is that I am unable to verbalize it. I just don't want others to suffer like I did. Am I wrong to think this way?*

He finally got out of the classroom and was walking through the corridor when he received a message from Ruhi.

I am always with you and you'll find me by your side, but only as long as you are right. And let me say this, you have already started a walk in the opposite direction. Frankly, I don't know for how long I can be with you, but till you disappear from my eyesight, you will find me standing behind you. I have truly loved you and cannot see you get hurt. But the path you have chosen for yourself is sure to hurt you. I tried my best to stop you but failed. Now, the longevity of our relationship depends on your actions and I'll pray to God that you emerge not only victorious but honourable too. Love you, Raghu.

Ruhi kept her mobile aside and lay on her bed thinking how life had treated them in the past few months and how things had changed drastically. She had a sinking feeling in the pit of her stomach and suddenly, she couldn't hold back her tears. As she closed her eyes, she realized that Jai was probably right in the way he had chosen to bring back Raghu—his friend and her one true love. Her phone beeped; it was him.

I won't let you down, breaking your faith and leaving you hurt. Love you too, Ruhi.

'Krishna, when will the final list of candidates be declared?' Raghu asked during an AISC meeting being conducted in one of the hostels. It was an informal meeting where only senior students showcasing leadership qualities had been called. Raghu loved the attention and respect he got at such meetings.

'It should be out next week. The committee scrutinizes students who have filled out the forms and then decides the final names after filtering the rest,' Krishna said as he stood leaning on the wall. 'Comrades, we still have enough time on our hands and we should remember that our fight is for the poor and their rights. Let's never forget this lest we get side-tracked during campaigning; we will preserve the MGU culture.'

Everyone was tuned in to the discussion, suggesting ideas and better ways of implementation of those ideas. As the session progressed, Raghu started feeling a little uncomfortable with the points being raised. Everyone was just discussing the strategy to *win* rather than a strategy to *build a better future*.

Sensing Raghu's discomfort, Krishna piped in, 'Raghu, I know it's your first time and I see that you're nervous. Listen, don't think too much about it. Just remember the larger cause we are fighting for—the betterment of the poor, and we have to win these elections if we have to do something for them. With no power, we won't be able to execute a single policy. And to win any battle, you need to have a plan of action. Understand? Here, have a drink to cool down.' He flung a bottle of beer to him.

'No, I'm good,' Raghu replied, placing the bottle on the ground, still apprehensive about the whole thing.

One after the other, different strategies were presented. Every detail revolved around how to emerge victorious—even if it was through unethical means. Krishna, however, had the best strategy of all.

'As we all know, the first-year admission process has begun in full-swing. There are around 600 rooms in the hostel campus for around 1400 students out of which some will be new admissions. If you do the math, you will see no one gets a separate room and every room will have two to three people in it. All the members of our organization who get new admissions as room partners need to act as parasites—keep them as close to you as possible and win them over slowly so that they vote for us at the upcoming elections.'

Raghu was shocked at Krishna's modus operandi. *Brainwashing the minds of innocent newcomers! Was I brainwashed similarly? Did Krishna win me over with lies as well? Was Jai actually right?*

The meeting broke up, but Raghu continued to be haunted by his doubts. He had promised Ruhi that he wasn't going to do anything that would make her feel ashamed of him. Was he about to break his promise? He pushed these thoughts away and went to the college playground where Krishna was due to deliver a speech to a group of students.

On the way, Raghu met Krishna. 'Remember, you're doing it for your own people. You have to win to secure their rights,' Krishna mumbled to him.

Once there, Krishna lost no time and immediately began his address to the gathered students. 'Salaam, students of MGU. The time for elections is near and we need your support in our fight for the poor and the downtrodden. We have always been discriminated against and we won't let that happen. If the poor are given anything, it is termed as subsidy but when the rich get anything, it is termed as incentives. We won't let this happen . . .'

The speech went on for an hour and while a certain section of the audience cheered him on, there were some who booed him and posed some pertinent questions. One such question caught Krishna unaware.

'If you want our vote, can you tell us one thing you have done for the betterment of the poor?' It was Jai. He had come to listen to the speech along with Chris.

For the first time, Krishna was at a loss for words. He quickly changed the topic and ended the speech within the next few minutes.

Chris stood there smiling. 'What a liar and a hypocrite!' he whispered to Jai.

'No surprises there,' Jai replied. His eyes were transfixed on Raghu who in turn stood watching Krishna and then looked straight at him. Krishna had no answer to Jai's question but his silence gave Raghu his much-needed answer.

Election mania was on in full swing in the MGU campus. On one hand, the AISC and ABCP were leaving no stones unturned to ensure a win, while on the other, the SCI, a much smaller party than the other two, was giving them a tough fight with their impassioned speeches. The SCI's presidential candidate, Akhilesh, had created quite a stir in the college campus with his demand for a 24/7 library for girls too. But Krishna did not feel threatened. He was confident that all it would take was one provocative speech and students would be lured to his side. His movement, Kraanti, continued and Raghu was now one of his favourites. He was promoted as assured and controlled tasks assigned to him. He even got an appreciation letter after successfully delivering literature books a couple of days after Krishna's speech. Even the ABCP, which usually lay low during elections, now surfaced with a new face. With Jai, Chris, and Megha at the helm of affairs, the party was now seen as a strong contender, making the elections a game of equal power to watch keenly.

An ABCP meeting was in progress in the campus.

'Do you think your idea will yield the desired results? I personally feel it's a little risky,' an ABCP representative said to Jai. 'Plus, we need to talk with the regional heads for funds. We're running out of cash and can't go on functioning like this.'

'I understand but we need to change the way people think about us and the way we function. We need to overhaul our previous image of being an overly aggressive party and show the students that we truly care for their well-being. Fortunately, with Megha leading us, we have the women's votes for sure,' Jai said.

'That's not a given, Jai. Women can just as well vote for a male candidate,' Megha snapped.

'True, but we still stand a better chance of winning with you leading us.'

'Fine, I'll discuss with the national head about it,' the ABCP representative finally said.

Jai prepared a press release, assuming he would get a positive response from the national head of ABCP. And he was right—they gave a go-ahead to the idea he had put forth in the meeting. The gears had shifted—now there wasn't much time and they had a lot of work to do.

Jai told Chris to send the press release to all major media outlets so that it could be covered in the papers the following day. Although fairly confident, he and Megha were still a little nervous about the whole thing and whether their plan would unfold the way they planned.

'The press release has been sent,' Chris said pressing the send button on his laptop.

'Great. So we still have a couple of days to plan the whole thing out. Also, after the media coverage, we will find out what's on the minds of the students.'

'We should only target the area surrounding MGU in the beginning,' Megha suggested.

'I agree, so let's start from there,' Jai added.

$\mathcal{L}$

The next day, and for a number of days thereafter, the ABCP was all over the news.

'ABCP has decided to protest against the recent series of tax hikes by the Delhi state government. It will be a peaceful protest that will start and end at Jantar Mantar. The protest is being led by Megha, the party's presidential candidate from MGU for the upcoming elections. They have assured that there would be no public loss . . .'

Jai and Megha were drinking tea in the campus canteen and watching the news being played on TV. Every now and then, a student would come up and have a casual chat with them. The positive reaction from everyone was an encouraging sign.

It was the day of the protest, and Jai, Chris and Megha were all set for action.

Akhilesh and Krishna weren't too fazed by the ABCP hogging all the limelight. They had conducted similar protests in the past and were certain that a protest like this would have little impact on people. It was around noon when the ABCP representatives who were assembled at Jantar Mantar gave a go-ahead for the march. Once considered a historical hotspot, Jantar Mantar was now the unofficial designated protest site in the capital.

A huge section of the media had turned up to cover the event live. Jai, Chris and Megha were leading the protest from the front. A few minutes into the march and the sea of protesters divided itself into two groups. One headed by Megha made its way to liquor shops, while the other group led by Jai and Chris went in search of cigarette shops. As Megha stopped at a liquor shop with her followers in tow, the shopkeeper greeted her with a huge smile plastered on his face. 'Good afternoon, ma'am,' he wished.

'We'll buy everything. Pack up the whole thing,' she instructed her team.

'Everything?'

'Yes, and send me the bill and I'll have it settled. Don't leave even a single bottle,' Megha ordered.

Journalists who had followed her into the shop looked at each other with quizzical expressions on their faces. The shopkeeper did as he was told and drew up a total bill of three lakhs! The media and the shopkeeper himself stood there, stunned. Jai and Chris had similarly instructed their team to buy all the cigarettes they could find in all shops nearby.

Finally, the entire collection of bottles and cigarette packs were taken to an open ground and the heap was set on fire. Everyone, including the media, was left speechless. Once the fire died, Megha finally revealed her reasons behind the act. She wanted to make a statement about increasing taxes on commodities such as cigarettes and alcohol instead of hiking it for essential items. As promised, the ABCP had carried out the entire protest without troubling even a single person; they had broken through their old image of being an aggressive party with an exemplary peaceful march. And just as they had hoped, they won themselves a big fan following.

Megha became a star overnight. Every news story and TV discussion on the subject had her on the screen—the mastermind behind the grand plan. Everyone sang her praises and even the higher authorities of ABCP appreciated her efforts. Jai, on the other hand, couldn't be happier at being successful in executing the entire act peacefully. In other parts of the campus, the AISC and the SCI realized their mistake in underestimating the strength of the ABCP. Raghu was, however, happy that his friends' party was doing so well and sent Jai a congratulatory message. Jai's response was curt and sounded more like a taunt,

Always standing by the right, bro! At the end of the day, only one person can emerge victorious. But it should be by the right means. Just a little sad that a few people don't realize it. But I am sure they will before it's too late.

Over the next few days MGU turned into a campaigning fortress. Jai's plan started taking root as Raghu's doubts became stronger. He could clearly see the difference between Krishna's and Jai's approaches towards the election. Everyone now waited anxiously for the final candidate list that was going to be announced very soon.

Fifteen

20 June 2016

'Did you read the newspaper? There's an article on Megha and how she's taking a stand against reservation,' Ruhi said as she came running towards Raghu to tell him the good news. Raghu simply nodded with an expressionless face. They were sitting in an empty classroom after the lectures for the day had ended.

Not paying heed to his unresponsiveness she continued, 'I still remember the day she had announced her candidacy on Facebook and Akhilesh sent her a warning to remove the post. Today, she is kicking his ass. Woohoo, go Megha!'

'Ruhi . . . please stop,' Raghu replied with a heavy voice.

'I so agree with her. I don't know about betterment but all I know is this whole drama around caste and religion creates a tiff between the best of friends.'

Raghu remained quiet. Ruhi noticed that he was not his usual self. 'What's wrong? Are you okay?' She went closer to him.

He was not. And he had no idea what he was doing. As the ABCP, with their righteous approach, kept getting popular, Raghu's doubts over his decision to be with the AISC grew stronger. It seemed to him that the party was all talk, no show. He wanted to talk to Ruhi about it, but something stopped him. *What if she took it the wrong way?*

'Are you okay?' Ruhi asked again, shaking him out of his stupor.

He looked deep into her eyes and before she could say anything, grabbed her close and kissed her passionately. Ruhi was taken by surprise. As they broke away from the kiss, Raghu whispered into her ears, 'I so needed this . . . I love you. You don't know what you mean to me.' And before she could say anything, he began grazing her neck, planting small kisses everywhere.

'Raghu . . .' she sighed in ecstasy. 'We can't do this here. It's a classroom . . .'

But he cut her short as he devoured her mouth. Unable to hold back any longer, Ruhi threw her arms around his neck and responded to his caresses with equal fervour.

A few minutes into their sudden make-out session, Ruhi finally broke free. 'I have to leave. I have some urgent work to attend to.'

Before Raghu could stop her, she hastily collected all her things and dashed out of the classroom. He lay there thinking about her, how good she was to him and how deeply he loved her. In her company, he forgot all about his problems. Her warmth gave him comfort, the comfort he craved for ever since the campaigning had picked up speed and he had found himself feeling lost and alone.

It was Sunday evening and Jai was sitting at the roadside dhaba along with Chris and Megha. Typically for that time of the week, all the hot girls of MGU sauntered along the road in their prettiest outfits. 'You know what my ultimate goal before graduation is?' Chris asked while checking out the girls.

'To lose your virginity?' Jai replied cheekily.

Megha laughed.

'What the fuck do you mean? I am very respectful of girls. My ultimate goal is to have at least one serious relationship before I pass out. Otherwise, I have to be content with watching movies like *Kuch Kuch Hota Hai* and *Rehna Hai Tere Dil Mein*.'

'The possibility of the latter happening is more likely.'

'Hey! I am talking about my emotions and here you are making fun of me!'

'I'll help you get laid after I win the elections and become president.' Megha smirked.

'Spoken like a true friend. Just send all the girls in your party to me and I'll help solve all their problems.' Chris winked back at her.

Jai laughed and was about to place an order for a cup of tea when he saw a couple of bikes positioned at the far end of the road. He looked around and saw some guys come out of the adjoining building, get on those bikes and ride away. Although he had caught only a glimpse, Jai was sure they were the same guys who had once tried to harass Megha on the road.

'There they are! I've been looking for them for far too long. This is it.'

'Are you sure?' Chris asked.

'I'm certain of it! I can never forget those faces. Last time I missed nabbing them, but not today. Come with me, Chris,' Jai commanded as he ran out and kick-started his bike. Megha tried to stop the two, saying it wasn't worth it, but Jai had made up his mind and ignored her plea.

'But we have to be careful,' Chris advised as he took up a seat behind his friend.

As they rode towards the direction of the bikes, Chris instructed, 'Just keep riding and try to overtake them at some point. And when we cross paths, don't look at them or else they'll get suspicious.'

A few minutes of chasing and Jai picked up speed around a U-turn. He eventually overtook them and stopped his bike abruptly in front of them. One of the two bikers sensed something was wrong and sped away but the other one couldn't escape. Both Jai and Chris pounced on him and beat him black and blue. By the time people had gathered to see what the commotion was all about, it was over.

Realizing that the elections were closing in and he and Chris were friends of the presidential candidate, Jai decided to spare the guy on the condition that he wouldn't repeat his act in the future.

But just like he had thought, the ABCP was not at all pleased on hearing about the incident. Jai apologized to the team for his actions and promised not to do anything of this sort in the future—or at least till the elections were over. Megha, however, was bowled over by Jai—once again. That he had cared so much for her that he would take such a risk despite knowing it was against the ethics of the ABCP endeared him to her even more.

21 June 2016

It was the day the final list of candidates was going to be declared. All the candidates and their respective supporters had gathered near the main bulletin board at the college entrance where the list was going to be put up. Surprisingly, Krishna was nowhere to be seen. In fact, no one had seen him all morning and his supporters looked lost without him.

'So, Ms Megha, how are you feeling right now?' Jai teased her.

'It's scarier than exam results and I don't think I've ever been more nervous in my life!' Megha replied, rubbing her hands in nervousness.

'You're a winner for us, regardless of the list,' Chris said reassuringly.

Raghu and Ruhi were standing at some distance from them, but every now and then, Raghu cast a glance at his former friends. He could see they were as nervous as he was about the results. After weeks of campaigning, the final list of candidates was going to be announced soon.

After an hour-long wait, the list was finally put up. A heavy crowd gathered around the board in eager anticipation. Jai and Megha pushed through the gathering and made their way to the front. Scanning through the list, they tried to locate Megha's name on it. It was not there. Thinking they may have missed it somehow, their fingertips scanned the names once again. That's when it hit them.

Megha's name was missing in the final list because she had been rejected!

'How the fuck is this possible? It's a fucking conspiracy, Megha! We must do something about it. They just can't reject you like this. I mean what was the basis of the rejection?' Chris yelled.

Rallying behind him, ABCP supporters started screaming in protest, demanding the results be re-checked. Jai wondered if he was the reason behind the shocking rejection since he had gone against the party ethics when he beat up the biker. But then he had apologized to the ABCP for his action, so that couldn't be it.

In contrast, the AISC and SCI supporters were rejoicing. Both their candidates—Krishna and Akhilesh—had made it to the list. But Raghu found it strange that Krishna was missing from the scene. *Could Krishna have been involved in manipulating the final list?* Raghu dismissed his thought as quickly as it came to him. No one, in the history of the elections, had been able to manipulate the list.

Meanwhile, Jai and his teammates regained their composure and went to the selection committee room where its members were just returning from the boardroom.

'How could you just reject Megha's form? She did nothing wrong,' one of the head representatives of ABCP asked the panellists furiously.

'We have no personal grudges against anyone. The list says all we have to say on this matter.'

They did not argue too much and instead handed over Megha's application form to her. She opened it in fear and saw that every criterion had been met except one. That made her even more furious.

Lack of attendance in Mrs Nair's classes. The candidates need to meet the 75 per cent attendance criterion for each subject, in the absence of which the form will be rejected.

But how could it be? Megha asked herself. She clearly remembered that one day when she had to skip her class halfway through because of her headache. But she had thought Mrs Nair would mark her present for a class upon her request.

'It's just one class. Does it matter so much?' Jai asked the committee, raising his voice in frustration.

'Yes, it does. Mrs Nair has taken all of three lectures this year and if she is absent for one, her attendance for that class goes down to 66.6 per cent. I think that clears up everything. Now can you please leave?' one of the committee members replied curtly.

Megha, Jai and the head representative were left speechless by the decision, and left the room in anger.

'I had a severe migraine that day and after taking permission from Mrs Nair, I excused myself from the class. She even announced in front of the whole class that I shouldn't worry about the attendance and leave. I assumed she would remember to mark me present. Ruhi was there with me that day—she will remember,' Megha recounted as they made their way out.

Jai put his arm around Megha in consolation and asked her not to worry about it too much. He was about to say something else when he noticed Krishna passing through the corridor with a smug expression on his face. And he wasn't alone; Mrs Nair was with him!

That's strange! What is Krishna doing with Mrs Nair when he should be out with his teammates by the bulletin board? I must get to the bottom of this, Jai thought to himself

Megha's sobs broke his train of thoughts. 'I'm sorry. I should have attended the lecture,' she cried. She then walked over to her fellow party members and apologized for not having lived up to their expectations. They didn't know how to react; it was a big setback for the party. In another part of the college campus, Raghu went to Krishna to give him the good news but stopped dead in his tracks when he saw him leading Mrs Nair into a room. The cloud of confusion was finally lifting off Raghu's eyes. He remembered his first session of AISC when Mrs Nair had addressed the students. Krishna had tried to outwit them all!

But what could he do? He had no proof. And at that point, no one would have listened to him anyway. Or so Raghu thought, and kept mum.

Dejected and heartbroken, Megha retreated to her room and asked everyone to keep away. She wanted to be left alone for some time. The rejection was not going to affect her in the long term, but the way things had played out depressed her completely. She realized that she had been made the scapegoat of a larger conspiracy. She failed her party, she failed herself, and what about Raghu? Now they would never be able to set their plan in motion to bring their friend back.

With a heavy heart, she logged on to Facebook and wrote,

It's all fabrication—the list, the names of candidates, the selection procedure, everything. Yes, I am hurt. Why shouldn't I be? Even I have emotions. But that does not mean I have given up. That does not mean the people who are behind this conspiracy have won. My motive to join politics was not to gain anything material from it. It was to gain back a lost friend. And we won't give up until we have succeeded in doing just that. We will come back stronger and fight harder than ever for our cause. Satyameva Jayate.

Sixteen

22 June 2016

'Congratulations, comrades. We've taken our first step towards victory . . .' Krishna addressed the AISC party members.

Then he went around to Raghu and said, 'Today I'm assigning you your biggest task yet. On the face of it, the task might look easy, but it isn't. The NGO people to whom you're supposed to deliver the parcels today come under the high-risk bracket. That's the reason I don't want any other student except you to handle it. This is a big task, the biggest till date for you.'

'Why is it high-risk?' asked Raghu.

'Because it's a decider. It'll decide the fate of thousands of poor Dalits and people from other lower castes; it'll decide the results of the student elections which are not far. It'll decide our fate. This time you have to bring back another bag along with you and hand over a note with the parcel. Upon arrival, you have to deliver the bag to a firm in Delhi.'

Raghu listened carefully as Krishna continued, 'The higher authority will keep an eye on you for your safety.'

My safety? Raghu wondered. Something didn't feel right about the whole thing. But he didn't want to outwardly refuse to do the job because that would mean arriving at a dead end. If he had to get to the bottom of what was happening, he had to play along. After discussing with Krishna further, he agreed.

With the traumatizing memories of Ambala still lingering in his mind, Raghu began his journey to the heartland of Haryana in the wee hours of the night. After a couple of hours, he reached the Good Luck restaurant, where the meeting was scheduled to take place. But the restaurant was completely deserted, with not a person in sight. Raghu waited for more than an hour, looking around, hoping someone would turn up, but no one came.

In the meantime, Ruhi kept calling him on his phone but he ignored the calls, focused solely on the job at hand. Eventually, he decided to cut open the parcels to check if it was safe to leave them there. All this while, his phone kept ringing. Before he could cut open the parcel, he decided to pick up the call.

'I need to tell you something like right now,' Ruhi shouted from the other side; she sounded worried.

'Not now, Ruhi. I will call you tonight, I am a little busy.'

'I know! But I need to tell you—'

Before she could finish her sentence, Raghu disconnected the call.

Keeping his phone back into his jeans pocket, he cut open one of the boxes. The contents in the box brought his life to a screeching halt. It was stuffed with bundles of cash! He tore open another box and another—they all confirmed his worst fears! He realized that Krishna's movement, Kraanti, was not about helping the poor but about feeding the powerful. All their big talk and big ideas were nothing but hogwash. As he gathered the scattered bundles and dumped them back into the bags, he tore open the envelope and read the message inside:

Hope the material this time is of better quality and not like last time when we targeted the DLF Mall area near MGU for the riots. Your money is safe in the boxes.

Raghu couldn't believe what he was reading. Krishna was behind the DLF Mall attacks? The incident which caused a rift with his friends and put Ruhi's life in danger? And he was supporting the very person who was responsible for it? Raghu felt choked. He had barely regained composure when a car entered the restaurant compound. *It must be one of his guys coming to collect the money*, Raghu thought. As if the latest disclosure did not jolt him enough, another shock awaited him. Raghu had to pinch himself to believe what he saw in front of his eyes.

It was Chris who stepped out of the car, which was filled with the same boxes as Raghu's.

As Chris came and stood in front of Raghu, all he managed was a hoarse 'Why?'

Chris had no answer to Raghu's question.

'You guys held me guilty for changing parties, but you are no different from me. All this while you've been working for Krishna as well? Why did you backstab Jai and Megha? They trusted you, and what did you do in return? Made fools of their trust? Why, Chris? Answer me!'

Chris kept his head down like a schoolboy caught stealing in a candy store by his father.

'Have you lost your mind? Give me a fucking answer! When did you get involved in such nefarious activities?' Raghu kept prodding but Chris wouldn't say a word.

'Do you even know what's in the boxes? Since the first day of my joining, I've been delivering these parcels without knowing about their contents. Do you know the very same people who ask me to transport these boxes are also the ones behind the DLF Mall riots?' He handed over the note to Chris.

'So the mystery is getting solved,' Chris finally said, but without giving any justification about his presence, or his level of involvement with Krishna and his organization.

'But give me more information. Where exactly are you coming from?'

'From another location where I delivered some boxes and collected a few bags as per instructions. I got to know about the money racket during my last task, and today, when I took up another task, I checked the bags on an impulse and found weapons inside.'

'Oh fuck. These people are monsters and want nothing but power. Red salute is not about all this. Krishna is a monster.'

'Yes, it's a power game in which we have become embroiled. These kinds of people manipulate us on false grounds and use us for their benefit. But let's not say or do anything in haste. Or you never know what will happen—'

As if out of nowhere, another car appeared on the scene. A few burly-looking men got down and instructed the two to keep the bags in their car's boot. Raghu handed over the boxes from his car to them, after which they left. The two friends decided that Raghu should complete his task of delivering the bags to the firm in Delhi before they revealed anything to anyone. They had to be very careful, lest anyone from Krishna's camp got a whiff of their intentions. Raghu knew that he had broken Ruhi's trust completely, but Chris's involvement shocked him even more. Heavy-hearted, he returned.

The same day, a few minutes earlier

Ruhi was passing through the lecture hall after finishing her classes when she reached the ground floor and saw Krishna going into one of the classrooms along with someone she couldn't quite place but knew was a part of Krishna's movement. She followed the two and saw that the door had been shut. Nevertheless, she pressed her ear against the door and listened intently. 'You have assigned such a huge task to two relatively new members of the organization. You think they are reliable?' the senior representative asked Krishna apprehensively.

'Yes, both are very naive and will do whatever I tell them to without asking too many questions. Moreover both have been victims of discrimination.' It was Krishna's voice—calm and confident.

After a pause, he added, 'Don't worry. Raghu will deliver the boxes of money as well as the weapons without knowing what he is actually carrying.'

'What next?'

Ruhi's jaw dropped. She retreated to a corner and frantically dialled Raghu's number. But he kept disconnecting her calls. In her repeated attempts to call him, she missed a part of the conversation inside the classroom.

'We don't need them after the next task. So you know what has to be done, right?'

'You mean make them go "missing", just like we did with Mani?'

'Exactly.'

'But will that be a wise option, considering all the chaos created after Mani went missing? What if the trail leads back to us?'

Krishna was the mastermind behind the missing-student case! So crafty was the execution that even the Delhi Police got no leads, and the case went cold. Hiding behind the veil of ideologies of the AISC, Kraanti was all about manipulating students on the grounds of religion, using them for personal gains and then getting rid of them with the support of political big guns.

Ruhi could feel her head spinning as she desperately tried to call Raghu from the college corridor. *Fuck man, please pick up. This is serious. Raghu, you are risking your life,* she thought to herself.

After numerous attempts, she gave up and went running back to hear the rest of the conversation. But she had already missed the major parts.

'You don't need to worry on that account. Just a little more time and Raghu will be the next one,' said Krishna.

'You mean . . . Are you serious, even after so much of chaos?'

'It's not me who has decided it. Also, he's not going to be facing it alone.'

'Then?'

'Both of them,' the voice confirmed.

There was some mumbling and then it was Krishna's voice again, 'You don't need to worry on that account. The orders are from higher up. Both Raghu and—'

Suddenly, sounds of footsteps rang through the corridor. Ruhi hurriedly made an exit lest she get caught. After reaching a safe distance, she stopped to catch her breath. She couldn't hear the second name. But one thing was clear—Raghu's life was in grave danger. She made one last attempt to call him. This time he picked up her call, only to disconnect immediately after saying that he was busy. Ruhi had to tell someone all she had heard. And the only other person she relied on after Raghu was Megha.

She called her up and said that she had something important to tell her. Megha asked her to come directly to her room. Ruhi reached there in no time, sweating profusely. Megha made her sit on the bed and gave her a glass of water.

'What happened? Is everything all right?' she asked anxiously.

Ruhi narrated all that she had seen and heard, trying to recollect as best as she could.

'This is unbelievable. And they call themselves honourable students!' Megha was both shocked and disgusted. 'Raghu should expose them rather than supporting them in their actions. What is wrong with him? Can he not differentiate between good and bad?'

'People like Krishna are not here for studies. They are bloody sleeper cells working to disrupt the environment whenever ordered. They stay in college for years under the pretext of a PhD thesis when their agenda is just to stay on and brainwash students into believing them and their ideology,' Ruhi said bitterly. 'Like Raghu, they might have manipulated so many students over the years for their own political gains. It's a huge racket that needs to be exposed. But I'm not fearless enough to do it. I'd rather stay away from all this, finish my studies and leave the university rather than get involved and spoil my future,' she admitted.

'Whatever,' Megha said, equally upset. 'Raghu was foolish enough to get involved in all this. We had warned him so many times, you know that for a fact. Jai decided to get into all this mess just to save him. We didn't want to have anything to do with the elections. We were leading ordinary lives as students.'

Ruhi kept quiet, unsure what to say or do next.

'You know why my form got rejected? Because of Krishna,' Megha said.

'Really? How do you know?'

'I saw him walking into a classroom with Mrs Nair.'

'Mrs Nair?'

'Yes, remember we walked out of her class? The reason for my candidacy rejection was cited as low attendance in her class. I'm certain Krishna made her mark me absent for the class on purpose.'

'That bitch! But frankly, I'm not surprised. I always expected something this low from Krishna. Raghu broke my trust,' Ruhi's voice quivered. 'So what happens next?' she asked, regaining her composure. 'Do you fight against the committee and ask for a hearing?'

'I don't know. ABCP representatives are trying to figure it out. Possibly by tomorrow we will get a clearer idea.'

'This is downright dirty. As if Krishna cleared the 75 per cent attendance rule.'

After spending some time with Megha, Ruhi felt a little better. She decided to keep trying to get in touch with Raghu. Eventually she would succeed. And she couldn't give up just yet.

✦

Even after Ruhi left, Megha couldn't stop thinking about what she had heard. Neither Jai nor she could imagine something of this magnitude had been taking place right under their noses!

But there was a crucial part missing—the identity of the second person whose name Ruhi did not hear. Megha kept wondering who that could be. She was restless all through the night and couldn't catch a wink. Her fatigue was evident when she met Jai the next day.

'You look tired,' he commented as she walked up to him. She narrated the entire story to him. 'I knew it! I knew Krishna couldn't be trusted,' he said, shocked nonetheless.

'But what do we do now? How do we show his lying face to the world? Now we can't even stand for elections.'

'What baffles me is that they have managed to trap the professors too. There has to be a way out of this mess.'

'What if we are underestimating the professors' role in all this? What if they are more deeply involved?'

'No. That's not possible. After all, they are professors in a reputed institution. They wouldn't dare to do something like this for fear of tainting their holier-than-thou image. No organization or institution would support such acts, but because of people like Krishna the entire organization is blamed. How I wish we could lead normal lives again. How I wish I could snatch Raghu from their vicious clutches,' Jai lamented.

Megha came closer and put a hand on his shoulder. She had never seen him get so emotional.

'You are doing whatever you can. I am always there for you. And so is Chris,' she tried consoling him.

'I used to fight with Raghu, but only because he was such a good friend; our debates, our arguments, they were all for fun. It was never my intention to hurt him. He is my brother. My best friend. I feel so helpless right now. These people are criminals and I am sure they might have tricked many innocent minds into believing them. What are they doing with them?'

'Do you think Raghu knows the truth about Krishna and is still a part of his organization?'

'I'm sure Raghu is trapped and the truth has to come out.'

'Did ABCP make progress with regards to the election? They had asked for a couple of days' time,' Megha asked in anticipation.

'Yes, they are meeting us in some time. But I wouldn't get my hopes up.'

Just then, a senior representative from ABCP came running towards them. 'Jai! I have great news. We are back on track!'

Jai looked at him with a confused expression on his face.

'Remember I had told you to fill out the form for covering candidate?'

'Yes, I remember. What about it?'

'In elections, the covering candidate is the one who takes over if the main candidate is rejected. They scrutinize the person's records and declare him or her as the presidential candidate in case the main candidate's nomination is rejected.'

'Are you serious? That's awesome!'

'Yes! So anyway the point is, your form has been approved and you are now the official candidate for the party. The reason why we told you to fill out the form and not anyone else is because we knew Krishna wouldn't have expected this coming. He would have expected us to get some regular ABCP student to cover, someone he could have easily plotted against. But he wouldn't have anticipated this. You are the question that came out of syllabus.'

By then, a number of other party members had arrived, rejoicing at last. Megha was relieved and more than happy, but Jai still looked disappointed.

'Aren't you happy?' Megha asked him.

'I would have been, only if I wanted to be the president willingly. I thought you were deserving of the nomination and eventually the post because you have such a fan following. I am a nobody. Why will anyone in their right mind want to vote for me? With you we had a shot at winning. But not with me.' Jai sounded dejected.

'Oh, please. I'm no sensation,' Megha said with a wave of her hand. 'Everyone in the campus knows that you were the brain behind the tax hike act. So don't back out now, when we have finally found a way to bring Raghu back.'

Jai was still a little apprehensive. But after much coaxing from his team, he finally gave in and agreed to be the official candidate for the student elections. Jai and Megha hugged each other—they finally had a reason to smile.

After finally managing to get in touch with Raghu, Ruhi decided to meet him at a café. She couldn't wait to tell him all that had transpired in his absence.

She reached before him and chose a corner table where they could talk in privacy. Just as she was about to dial his number, Raghu walked in.

'Hey, so sorry for being late,' he apologized. He went and sat on the chair opposite her very nonchalantly, pretending as if nothing had happened. Raghu did not want her to get embroiled in the whole thing, so he had decided to keep it a secret, not knowing the crazy journey she had been on the last few hours.

'Raghu, if you don't mind, can I ask you something?'

'Of course! You don't need to ask for my permission,' he smiled.

'What work does your organization Kraanti do?'

'What do you mean?' He hadn't seen that coming.

'I mean what's the motive behind its establishment?' She crossed her arms on the table and leaned ahead, carefully observing him while he answered.

'To help the poor. But you know that, so why are you asking me?' he asked uneasily.

'Are you sure?'

'Yes.'

'Either you are ignorant or feigning innocence,' she declared.

'Get to the point, Ruhi.'

'I heard Krishna talking to one of the representatives about the tasks assigned to you. I now know the real nature of your job,' Ruhi replied.

'What representative?' Raghu asked anxiously.

'It doesn't matter. For me, you and your safety is important. So tell me, for how long have you known?'

The secret was out and Raghu realized there was no point in hiding anything any more from her. 'To tell you the truth, I didn't know anything until yesterday, when I was on my task and you had called.'

This admission annoyed Ruhi even more. Even if it was for a day, he had hidden the truth from her.

'How can you act so indifferent? First you lied to me, and then never bothered to tell me what was going on!' she said, banging the table with the palm of her hand. The other diners stopped to look at them.

'Shhh, Ruhi, don't draw attention towards us. All this is still a big secret. So what do you want me to do? Go out and tell everyone out there in the university?'

'Yes, immediately.'

'You have lost your mind. I have no fucking proof! How can I announce everything to the world with no proof in hand? The whole thing will backfire on us.'

'Oh please, don't act like a coward.'

'I'm not. And if you think I'm a coward, then be happy with your assumption,' Raghu replied, trying to end the topic.

'Let me ask you very clearly. Are you going to confess the truth or not? You had promised to never do anything wrong, yet you've been actively involved in this whole thing since the very beginning. Still you act as if you are fucking innocent.'

'Cut the crap, Ruhi. Enough now,' Raghu said, losing his calm.

'I am giving you one last chance. Confess or else you lose me.'

Raghu didn't know what to say. What could he have said anyway? The truth was in front of him, but he refused to acknowledge it.

Ruhi got up from her seat to leave. But before she left, she decided to give Raghu a piece of her mind. 'You know what, Raghu? You have lost your friends, your self-respect and now you have lost me too. Don't expect me to stay with you any more. I can't be with someone who doesn't know right from wrong. I have one suggestion for you before I leave. Get out of this mess before it's too late. Once you're trapped, no one will be able to rescue you, even if you scream and shout.'

Raghu sat there staring at the café door. His only support had left him in the dumps. It wasn't long before his phone beeped with a message.

I had given all my love to you, but what did I get in return? Only a bunch of lies and fake promises. My heart is not a doormat on which you will keep wiping your feet. I gave you all my trust, but you misused it. I gave you the benefit of doubt, but you proved everyone right. I gave you my life, but you killed me slowly every single day.

His heart bled tears. He couldn't fathom a life without Ruhi. Without her around, everything seemed hollow and empty.

Seventeen

7 July 2016

A fortnight had passed since the day of their break-up. Raghu was sitting at an AISC meeting, looking dazed and confused. His thoughts kept wandering to Ruhi and the bitter note on which they had ended things. Lost, he didn't even realize when the meeting got over.

'Dude, it's been more than a week now. Get over it. Didn't I tell you such people always use us for their own benefit? She was no different, brother,' Krishna consoled him.

'What are you talking about?'

'Wasn't she a Brahmin, an upper caste? This love story could never have a happy ending,' he said, adding fuel to fire.

'That's not it. The reason for our break-up was something entirely different,' Raghu clarified.

'That doesn't matter. The point is, she has already moved on within a couple of weeks. And you should too. Take inspiration from her.'

'Who said she has moved on? It's just that . . .'

Krishna cut him short before he could finish his sentence. 'Raghu, you've been so lost ever since she broke up with you. Have you paid any attention to what was going on around you? Don't be an emotional fool. Voting day is inching closer. We hardly have a week's time left and there is a lot of work to be done.'

'What do you mean by that?'

'By what?'

'Lost . . .'

'Of course, open your eyes and see for yourself. A few days ago, our students spotted her with Akhilesh,' Krishna declared on a serious note.

'How's that possible?'

'You figure it out for yourself. But make sure that she doesn't reveal our tactics to him or I won't spare her.'

Raghu was sure Krishna was trying to play yet another trick on him, but this time he was not going to fall for his lies.

He decided to go look for Ruhi and clear the air once and for all. All through the search, he kept wondering why she would be with Akhilesh. *There's no reason for her to be with him at all. I could have still believed had he said she was seen with Jai or Chris, but Akhilesh? No, it seems unlikely. But what if she's trying to teach me a lesson by doing this? Damn, I need to clear this out.*

Ruhi was with a couple of girls from her class when Raghu spotted her and pulled her away from the group.

'Are you like . . . hanging out with . . . Akhilesh?' Raghu stammered out the words, but when he saw no reaction from Ruhi, he got irritated and asked further, 'Is there even the slightest hint of truth in this? If so, then I want an answer. When I got involved with the wrong people, you said all kinds of things to me, and now when you are with the wrong person, then what?'

'I am not answerable to you any more. So please leave me alone. If you don't, I will never speak to you in my life,' Ruhi replied in anger.

Raghu realized she meant what she said and loosened up. 'Why are you doing this to me? Please forgive me. Give me some time,' he tried again, gently.

'How much time do you need, Raghu? A lifetime? And who are you to question my actions when you couldn't even tell me why you lied? Please leave me alone.'

'Ruhi . . . please. Don't do this.'

'I am asking you to leave me alone. Is that so difficult to understand?' she shouted in frustration.

'It's been two weeks now, Ruhi . . . Please come back.'

'That's what, Raghu. It's been two weeks! But did you take any action? No, because you are a coward. So be one and let me live my life. Bye.' And saying so, she left.

Raghu stood motionless. Every word that Ruhi had uttered killed him from the inside. He had lost track of what he wanted. All he knew was that he loved her to the core.

Raghu finally made up his mind to expose Krishna in front of everyone the next time he was assigned a task. Whatever be the outcome, he didn't want to live a life filled with lies, a life without Ruhi. She had blocked him on all social apps, so he sent her a text message:

Ruhi, I have no excuse for what happened and my sorry holds no value. Today, when I looked into your eyes, I realized what I have done. You didn't have to say anything, I saw it all—betrayal, disillusionment, disgust. In that moment I just wanted to crawl under a rock somewhere and hide. I understand the gravity of what I've done, it's difficult for me to look in the mirror. I'm not proud of the person I see there. I have decided that I am going to take necessary action. I have just one request to you in all this. Please don't be with someone who can hurt you and leave you devastated. Yes, I am talking about Akhilesh.

Soon after, there was a beep on his phone. It was Ruhi:

I was once with a person who hurt me and left me devastated. No other person can hurt me more than him. Also, don't advise me on anything. You are not in a position to do so. When I came to know you supported the wrong person, I left you. Similarly, if you feel I am supporting the wrong person, you can simply block me.

Elections were just a week away and all parties were campaigning with full gusto. Jai and Megha along with the rest of the ABCP team had aggressively started promotional activities to highlight their good work and urged the students to vote for change. On the other side, Krishna was plotting strategically to ensure a win. Chris was somewhere in between—shouting slogans for Jai publicly while still working with Kraanti—the reason for which was still a big mystery to Raghu as Chris didn't even reveal a bit despite Raghu's insistence. His other concern was Ruhi's involvement with Akhilesh. Not only was he disturbed by it, he was also questioned about it by Krishna.

'And then you say politics doesn't interest you. Has anyone told you that you are best suited for politics?' Akhilesh smiled cunningly.

'Not more than you. All I know is that Raghu, Krishna and their party should not win these elections,' Ruhi declared.

'In the beginning, when you approached me saying you wanted to be a part of the SCI, I was surprised. I mean the entire college knew about your involvement with Raghu. Suddenly ditching him at the last moment was a master stroke!'

Ruhi and Akhilesh were sitting in the canteen after an SCI discussion meet. After parting ways with Raghu and her last meeting with Megha, Ruhi had taken a decision that shocked everyone. She had decided to support SCI in the upcoming elections. Obviously it didn't go down well with a lot of people, especially her friends. Jai distanced himself from her—even deleted her number from his phone. She joined Akhilesh's party despite knowing why Jai and Megha had stood for the presidential elections. Until then, all three of them were in it together, but now they had to part ways.

'Isn't it fair?' Ruhi said, taking a bite of her sandwich. 'As I had said, I don't care about anything other than seeing Raghu lose—not just the elections but his former friends and his love as well.'

'But what do you have against your other friends, Jai and Megha? You could have chosen to support their party,' Akhilesh asked. He was curious to know her reasons for choosing SCI.

'I could have. But after AISC, SCI is the second-most powerful wing in the campus. I can assure votes from the social science department where AISC has a stronghold. And I'd rather support a party that has a stronger chance of winning.'

Ruhi was playing a gamble by supporting Akhilesh. In truth, his victory didn't matter to her, but if SCI had a stronger chance of winning than ABCP, she'd rather support them to ensure AISC lost. Whatever may be the justification, neither Jai nor Chris had liked her move.

'I am speechless . . . We focused so much on Raghu and Krishna that we didn't realize Ruhi could pose us a threat at some point. And to think she was a friend. I can't believe she has stooped so low! In this war of showing Raghu right from wrong, we have lost many things,' Jai said in a tone of dejection.

They had assembled on the campus grounds where Jai was due to give a speech as part of the campaign.

'Have you seen Raghu recently? He's behaving very differently. I feel like he knows something but won't tell us. But we are on the right track. I'm hoping he can still see what's best for him and come around,' Megha replied.

'I don't think so. Is this what our friendship had to come to?'

'Jai, relax. You have to go on stage in the next few minutes. Look around, all the students are waiting to hear you speak; don't disappoint them.'

'Where is Chris? I haven't seen him since the morning,' Jai asked, looking around for him. He spotted Raghu in the crowd and they both exchanged an awkward smile.

'AISC students are shouting slogans against us, so he's gone to handle that.'

'That cannot stop me from speaking the truth.'

Jai knew it was his last chance to set things right. He mustered all the courage he had and spoke in a firm voice.

'Friends, we are here to bring about a change. Change in the thinking of the students. We think the whole reservation system should be abolished—it's time to start selecting on the basis of talent, education, hard work, experience and merit, irrespective of caste, class, gender, creed, age or income. Some of us want to play divisive politics and that's wrong. We are a secular state not because minorities demand it, but because the majority wants it. This secularism is in the DNA of our country and for the same reason, I say that I am a proud Hindu. And every person has this right to say that he is a proud Muslim, a proud Christian, a proud Sikh or a proud atheist. This is true secularism. Not abusing one religion or dividing people on the basis of religion. MGU is one family. We can never be intolerant, because it's not in the MGU culture. Our roots are built on the ideology of acceptance. And we will ensure that no one can uproot us! There's only one supreme power and that's of truth.'

The crowd broke into applause. Krishna was unnerved by the response. He knew he had to do something soon to save himself the humiliation of defeat. He had underestimated Jai's popularity and how good he was with words. Although he still considered himself a strong candidate, it was now evident that Jai was a big threat and could put an end to Kraanti .

Raghu, on the other hand, was already feeling remorseful for all that he had done. He wanted to confess everything to Jai but didn't have the courage to do so. No matter who won, he was the only student who had lost everything in this clash for power.

12 July 2016

'Were you able to record anything worthy, anything that can implicate them?' Raghu asked Chris on the phone. They had decided to collect proof in order to back their claim when they went public about Krishna's wrongdoings. With this, Raghu hoped to set a lot of things right, including winning Ruhi over.

'No, but Krishna has given me another task. What's strange is this time he's asked me to deliver the parcel alone and not collect any bags. Has he become suspicious of us?' Chris asked, sounding worried.

'He wouldn't have assigned you another task if that were the case. And I'm supposed to deliver a parcel too, so I think we're still in the safe zone here. Where are you delivering the parcels?'

'Ambala. And you?'

'Somewhere in Haryana, like last time,' Raghu answered.

'Did you manage to record anything?' Chris asked.

'Yes. But we'll talk about it later. It's not safe to divulge details on the phone. But do stay alert during the task. You never know when you get an opportunity to record something. Good luck,' Raghu said and hung up the phone.

After days of disillusionment and confusion, Raghu was now determined to gather all the scattered pieces of his life, and Chris was supporting him. Though Raghu wasn't successful in extracting the reason behind Chris supporting Krishna in his illegal acts, he was able to convince him to expose Krishna publicly. The next day, Chris began his journey to Ambala in the assigned car. He reached the delivery destination before sundown. A few minutes post his arrival, an Innova entered the delivery compound, and like always, Chris delivered the parcels kept in his boot and sat in the backseat without asking any questions. He messaged Raghu saying he was on his way back but had been unable to record anything. Clicking photos wouldn't have helped the cause as he knew they needed substantial proof to expose Krishna.

Raghu replied, *Don't worry, we will soon find tangible proof. Just delivered the parcels. On my way back now.*

Chris put the phone back in his pocket and thought about the last few days. Megha still didn't know of his involvement with the whole thing and he wondered how she would react once she found out. He would tell her it was important for him to get involved so deeply so that he could save Raghu from Krishna's clutches. Chris knew from the beginning that Krishna was just a pseudo-nationalist and thus, he had taken this route.

With a million thoughts racing in his mind, he didn't realize when he dozed off. An hour later when he opened his eyes, he looked out of the window and realized that the driver had taken a different route to Delhi.

'Why have you taken this route?' Chris asked. Something didn't seem right.

'Sir, I got a call from Krishna who instructed me to take this route since there were some security concerns on the main route.'

Chris wasn't convinced. He was familiar with the routes in that area and knew that the road they had taken was in fact longer and generally taken by truck drivers. He smelled something fishy.

'Krishna told you to take this route?' Chris asked nervously.

The driver turned around to answer, but before he could say anything, Chris saw a truck speeding towards them, head-on. 'Look out!' he screamed, but it was too late. Before they knew it, there was a huge collision and the car went flipping across the road, sending both Chris and the driver flying. Chris landed a few feet away from the car, his head oozing out blood, and specks of shattered glass all around him. He felt extremely dizzy, like the whole world was revolving around him. The driver was lying motionless a few metres away from him. Chris tried retrieving his phone from his pocket, but he was unable to move. He lay there crying out in pain. Finally, after repeated attempts, he caught hold of the phone and dialled Jai's number but before he could say anything, the phone fell from his hands. 'Can anyone hear me?' he cried feebly.

He wanted to run towards his friends—Jai, Megha, Raghu, Ruhi—but his body gave up and he lay there unconscious. Was it a tragedy or a planned strike? Whatever it was, he was pushed towards the doors of death.

Eighteen

Life had check-mated Chris but luckily, some passers-by spotted them and took them to the nearest hospital. The driver of the speeding truck had fled from the scene. Chris was taken to the emergency ward and the car driver was declared dead on arrival. One of the people who brought them in had the good sense to use Chris's phone and call the last dialled number to inform them about the accident. Luckily, it was Jai's number, and he left aside everything and rushed to the hospital with Megha.

'How's he? Is it very serious?' Jai asked as soon as he reached. The group of people who had admitted Chris in the hospital was patiently waiting outside his room.

'Don't worry. Catch your breath first,' one of them replied.

'What are the doctors saying?'

'He is out of danger. Luckily, we brought him well in time. Now that you are here, we'll take our leave.'

Jai and Megha heaved a sigh of relief. They thanked them for all their help and went to the on-call doctor to find out more about Chris's condition.

'He is lucky to have got away with a few injuries, considering the impact of the accident. You can meet him after a few hours, once he is well rested. Don't worry, he's a strong boy. So cheer up!' the doctor assured them.

'Thank you, doctor,' Jai said with folded hands and exited his room.

Outside, both the friends paced down the corridor impatiently. As they looked around, they saw a family crying over the death of their teenaged son; another was celebrating the birth of a baby. It made them think about the transitory nature of life.

'Do you want some water?' Jai asked Megha as she sat leaning her head against the wall.

'No. Do you?'

'It's okay. I'll help myself.'

Jai walked towards the cooler to get himself a glass of water but something was wrong with the nozzle. A hospital staff member directed him to another cooler that was working. As he walked towards that direction, he saw Ruhi; she seemed to be searching for a room. On seeing Jai, she burst into tears.

'What are you doing here?' Jai screamed.

'Calm down, Jai, it's a hospital, not your bedroom,' Megha chided him as she walked up from behind.

'I don't care. Just tell her to go away from here. I don't want to see her around me. We trusted her and she backstabbed us by joining Akhilesh's party. That's not what real friends do.'

'Will you please calm down? Don't forget we are here for Chris who is her friend too. She has every right to meet him. Why are you behaving like a school kid?' Megha tried calming him down.

'She can be a friend to no one. First, she betrayed Raghu and then us by joining a man who had once tried to harass you,' Jai replied.

'For God's sake, calm down. I am requesting you. You can at least respect my words, right?' Megha pleaded.

As they argued, Ruhi kept her head down, shame-faced. She knew that in Jai's eyes, she was at fault and that it was not the right time or place to explain her side of the story. So she preferred not to react to his allegations. Finally they all walked towards Chris's room. No one spoke a word to each other until the nurse came out of the room and announced that Chris was awake and that they could meet him. Everyone rushed inside and the moment they saw him, they let their emotions flow. Megha and Ruhi couldn't stop crying and held on to his hand tightly. 'I told you not to drink so much you, idiot,' Jai said in mock humour, concern lining his face.

'You know I don't drink.'

'That's why I told you to start drinking, you dumbass.'

Both of them grinned, and Jai came over to give him a hug. He didn't bother wiping his tears.

'We thought we had lost you,' Jai said, choked up.

'I am not going to die till I find myself a girlfriend. Remember my grand plan?' Chris winked. After a pause, he added, 'I want to tell you guys something before it's too late.'

'Not now. You need to rest,' Megha replied.

'No . . . I have to, otherwise god knows what might happen.'

'What is it, Chris?' Jai asked

'It was not an accident. Krishna planned the whole thing,' he stammered.

'How are you so sure?' Ruhi asked.

Chris explained how the driver had got sudden instructions to take a different route, how the collision had occurred from nowhere and how the truck driver conveniently made an escape before anyone could catch him.

'He wanted to kill me because . . .' Chris's voice trailed off.

'Because what?' Megha was getting impatient.

'Because I was posing a threat to his organization. I've been hiding something from all of you,' he said slowly. 'I've secretly been delivering parcels for Krishna illegally. Raghu is involved in this too. It's a big racket and now, since their work was done, they probably wanted to get rid of us.'

Megha lost her calm with this admission. 'Are you freaking serious? Even you?'

'You have every right to be angry with me. But hear me out completely first, please. I joined him because I knew that was the only way I could expose him. Raghu was so taken in by his ideologies! When Jai told me he suspected Krishna's involvement in a bigger scandal, I had to step in and do something myself. I won Krishna's trust over a period of time by attending his lectures and agreeing to whatever he said. But he deliberately kept me away from Raghu so that we didn't gang up against him.'

Jai, Megha and Ruhi listened on, too stunned to speak. Chris revealed every secret of Kraanti. 'Please save Raghu. He was delivering a parcel the same time as I was and I'm sure they want to get rid of him too. I really hope he's safe!'

Ruhi remembered the conversation she had overheard. So the second person was none other than Chris!

'Raghu knew you were involved, right?' Ruhi asked.

'Yes, but only recently, just before you broke up with him. He even told me he would get to the bottom of the whole thing because he made a promise to you.'

'Oh, please.'

'No, Ruhi, it's true. In fact, these past few days we've been looking for an opportunity to obtain some sort of proof against Krishna, but haven't been successful. Although, just before we left for our respective tasks, Raghu said he wanted to tell me something, but we decided on a later time since it was risky to do it over the phone.'

Ruhi felt guilty for having misunderstood Raghu. Never in her wildest dreams did she imagine it could cost him his life one day. Now she knew why he chose not to say anything on the matter. He had put his life in danger because he wanted to collect concrete proof against Krishna and his Kraanti first. Suddenly she felt a wave of concern for Raghu.

'I will never forgive myself for putting Raghu in harm's way,' she cried.

'Instead of discussing who's right and who's wrong, it'd be better if we save Raghu. His life is in grave danger,' Chris reminded them.

'Where could he be?' Jai spoke at last.

'Somewhere in Haryana. That's all I know. Go save him, guys, he needs you.'

'Where is Raghu?' Jai asked Krishna after spotting him at a dhaba a few metres away from the university.

'Why the hell are you asking me? Call him and ask him for yourself. I am sure you have his number,' Krishna stated arrogantly.

'Don't act like you don't know anything. Chris is in the hospital and you very well know why. So come out with it or we'll get it out of you. And what have you done with Raghu?' Jai asked in anger.

'Are you drunk? What are you talking about? Firstly, I have no idea why Chris is in the hospital, and secondly, how will I know where Raghu is? He is very much a part of the core group of AISC and he's a hard-working guy—we get along really well. So why would I do anything to him?' Krishna feigned innocence.

'Look, dude, I am warning you, if anything happens to Raghu because of you, I won't spare you.'

'Mind your language. You are a presidential candidate of the college,' Krishna retorted.

'Mind your actions. You too are one,' Jai replied and walked off.

Jai knew Krishna would not spill the beans so easily. There had to be another way out. He tried calling Raghu repeatedly, but his phone was switched off. Searching randomly all across Haryana was senseless, and would possibly be a waste of precious time. Jai went to Raghu's hostel to see if he'd returned, but he was nowhere to be found and his fellow hostellers had not seen him all day.

With a look of dejection, Jai returned to the college grounds where Megha was waiting for him. 'Did you check his Facebook or Instagram feed?' Megha asked as she logged on to her own Facebook account to see if there were any clues there.

'He has not posted anything since last week. Neither on Facebook, nor on Instagram. Not even on Snapchat,' Jai replied.

'Should we file a complaint with the police?' Megha could see no other option.

'No, that would simply add to the confusion. Also, we still don't know what Krishna has planned. I don't want Raghu to be in danger owing to a small mistake on our part.'

'While you were gone, Ruhi made calls to all the nearby hospitals to check if anyone named Raghu had been admitted recently, but that turned out to be a dead end as well,' Megha added in a feeble tone.

In another part of the campus, as she peeped into various classrooms looking for Raghu, Ruhi bumped into Akhilesh. 'I heard Raghu's gone missing? But why do you look so worried? It shouldn't bother you now that you guys have broken up,' Akhilesh said, rubbing salt on her wounds.

'Wow, what kind of logic is that? Whether we are in a relationship or not is none of your business. Just because I am a part of the SCI, I can't be dancing around to your tunes all day. Raghu is missing; whether he is a part of the

SCI or the ABCP or the AISC, I don't care. All I know is that a student of MGU has gone missing. When Mani went missing, did you celebrate, Mr Akhilesh?' Ruhi fumed in anger.

Akhilesh stayed tight-lipped.

'Don't you see a strange similarity in both the cases?' Ruhi asked.

'You mean AISC and ABCP are both involved?'

'Who said anything about ABCP? They were neither involved then, nor are they now. I don't know about AISC either,' Ruhi replied. She didn't know if she could trust Akhilesh with the information.

Raghu's sudden disappearance had stabbed Ruhi's heart and her conscience, and with each passing hour, she grew nervous and impatient. Slowly the news spread across the campus. Everyone had their own take. Some raised questions about Krishna, others pointed fingers at Jai and his team. Soon someone spread a rumour that Raghu was dead. Ruhi tried to look for the source of the rumour, but gave up soon after. She cursed herself for having mistrusted Raghu in the first place. Desperate, she kept calling on his number and although it was switched off, she sent him a message,

I don't know what to say other than that I am so sorry,
I truly am sorry. I took out all of my anger and hate on

you and I will hate myself forever for the way I treated
you. I am sorry that it took me so long to realize that.
I hurt you so badly and I didn't even see it. I pushed
you away to the point that you had to leave. We are
all worried for your safety, including Jai and Megha.
They love you. Come back—for them, if not for me. I
love you so much. Please come back.

The next day, Chris was discharged from the hospital. It was bad news for Krishna, but by then he had already politicized the news of Raghu missing in his favour. Within no time, he beat up the drum of discrimination and alleged in front of the crowds that it was the ABCP which was responsible for this. The party had plotted Raghu's disappearance since he had backstabbed its presidential candidate, Jai. And just like that, Krishna's master stroke right before the elections turned the wave of student favour to his benefit. Jai looked on helplessly, and both Megha and Chris could do little to comfort him.

The evening of 12 July 2016

Raghu was on his way back after completing his task and delivering the parcels to the designated location in Haryana. He was happy because he had finally managed to collect some proof against Krishna the other day—it wasn't incriminating evidence, but still, it was something. Now he could finally convince Ruhi of his love and that he had never intended to lie to her. He was merely a victim of circumstance who had unknowingly played into the hands of Krishna.

Raghu thought of calling Ruhi to give her the good news, but then decided against it. It would be way nicer if he told her in person. He looked out of the window, imagining his future with Ruhi—a future full of laugher and happiness. But his happiness didn't last very long. Suddenly, the driver stopped the car at a secluded spot. As if out of nowhere, a few men appeared on the scene, and after letting the driver go, they attacked the car with metal rods. They pulled out Raghu forcefully from the back seat and smashed his face with the rods, sending him tossing to the ground. He tried to get up in retaliation, but was too injured to do so. One of the men pulled him up and punched him in the stomach, and his head went banging on the car screen, shattering the windscreen.

'Who the hell are you? Leave me!' Raghu screamed.

'Just keep your mouth shut. Don't scream,' one of them threatened. They dragged him back inside the car and turned on the ignition.

'Where are you taking me?' he stammered.

Raghu could not comprehend what was happening. Dark memories of his last attack were still fresh in his mind. The man sitting in the driver's seat called up someone and said they were about to reach. Minutes later, they stopped outside a building and pulled Raghu out of the car. They made their way inside an apartment where a man was waiting to receive them.

'*You?* I knew you were behind this whole thing!' Raghu screamed. It was Krishna.

'Welcome, Raghu. I am so happy to see you,' Krishna smiled.

Before Raghu could understand what was happening, Krishna commanded the men, 'Come on, guys, let's give Raghu a special welcome. After all, he is my trump card.'

The men pounced on him and started beating him up. There was no way Raghu could have defended himself. He was bleeding and had bruises all over, but they continued hitting him, until Krishna told them to stop. He came closer to Raghu and threw a glass of water on his face.

'You know why you are here?'

Raghu could hardly speak, his lips were cracked.

'Because you will make me win the elections. You're my ticket to the presidential seat of MGU.'

Krishna told the men to leave the room and asked Raghu to sit on the chair kept in the centre.

'You have to do this for me,' he said, handing over some papers which he brought from the other room.

'What is it?' Raghu said feebly. His eyes were bruised from the beating and he couldn't make any sense of what was written on the papers.

'Your speech.'

'What?'

'You heard me. This is your speech that will help me win. You have to tell everyone in campus that some people tried to attack you and kill you just because you are from a lower caste and I came and saved you in the nick of time. You will acknowledge me as your life saviour in front of everyone and that'll make me a hero in the eyes of the students, who in turn will vote for me and make me the president of MGU. And that's how Kraanti will spread across the nation, in different universities.'

'You son of a bitch! You think I will do this? Never!' Raghu screamed.

'I am not asking you, I am ordering you to do this.'

'What if I don't agree?'

Krishna smirked. 'Chris, your friend? He must be dead by now. Accidental death, of course. Mani, the missing student, remember? Even he was involved with us, but like you, even he didn't agree to what I had said. The rest is history. Till date, no one has been able to trace him. There are big guns involved. I am just supporting them. Who knows what we'll do to your hot girlfriend if you don't agree to our demands. You know me well enough by now. If I can get rid of Chris, Ruhi should be easy to handle.'

'You bastard! What did you do to Chris? How could you? I won't spare you,' Raghu replied, agonized and angry.

'That's why I am telling you to be a good boy and do as I say. You'll be safe, your girlfriend will be safe, and you both can have a happily-ever-after.'

Raghu was scared for Ruhi. He understood that Krishna and his team could go to any length to get their work done.

Krishna said coolly, 'You will stay here for a day. I'm taking away your mobile phone—don't worry, I won't read any text messages from your girlfriend. Nor your sexts.'

'I'll kill you, you bastard.'

'First save yourself and Ruhi, and then you can plan to kill me. If you stay alive, that is. By the way, I love how much you love each other. I wish I could get a girlfriend like her.' Krishna laughed. He then continued, 'So I'll take you to the campus after a day, and you know what you have to do there. Hope I've made myself clear.' He handcuffed Raghu to the chair and left the room, locking the apartment.

Nineteen

14 July 2016

Raghu felt like his fate was sealed and there was nothing he could do. The complications of his life refused to reach a climax. He waited impatiently for hours in that small, dingy room with no windows or furniture. He was badly bruised from the fight and he felt his legs give way . . . yet sleep evaded him that night. When Krishna came to fetch him the next day, he was tired and groggy.

On their way to the college, Krishna reminded him about what he had to say. He had already concocted a story about Raghu's return in the university, saying he had saved his life.

Raghu had to make a decision once and for all. A decision that would affect all their lives. Jai's words rang in his head—*Someday someone will manipulate you.*

As their car entered the university gates, he was shocked to see students gather in large numbers to welcome him. Even in the midst of an ocean of students, his eyes searched for Ruhi but he couldn't find her. He just wanted to make sure she was safe. The moment he got down from the car, everyone hovered around him like he was a celebrity, chanting slogans like 'Raghu—you are our idol' and so on. Looking at them, he realized they were going to be fooled once again. He stood there completely baffled by the unexpected reception until his eyes fell on Ruhi who was standing at the far end. Slowly, he made his way towards her, pushing through the crowds.

'Ruhi . . . are you okay?' he asked.

'Where have you been all this while, Raghu? Everything's a complete mess. Do you know Chris was almost killed?'

'Almost? Oh that means he's alive! Thank god! Where is he?'

'He was hospitalized just in time. He's been discharged now. I don't know where everyone is but I am sure they must be here somewhere. We tried to look for you everywhere but your phone was switched off. Jai, Megha, we were all so worried. But what is all this about?' Ruhi asked pointing at the crowd.

'Krishna's behind it . . . it's scary . . .'

He turned around to see Krishna watching them from a distance. Raghu realized that any revelation at this point of time could prove lethal. He turned to face Ruhi and said softly, 'Just remember, I love you and I truly don't deserve you. I can never gain the same respect in your eyes again.'

'Don't say that. I sent you a message . . .'

'It is the truth. I am a coward. If only you knew why . . .'

Just then he heard Krishna call out his name. 'I have to go now, but I'll be back,' Raghu said, and walked back towards Krishna who handed over the mic to him.

Raghu glanced at him once and he gave him a nod to proceed with the whole thing as planned. He shut his eyes and took a deep breath.

What if I don't say what Krishna has asked me to and reveal the truth here? Will anyone believe me? And even if they do end up believing me, will they stand by me? What if Krishna does what he had threatened to do? No! I can't risk her life just because I want to prove something. I just can't. Raghu, do what he says, you have no option. You never had. What will Jai think? And Chris? No, Raghu! Krishna can do anything! Ruhi, I am sorry but I just can't let you suffer . . . I hope you find out one day that what I'm about to do is only and only for you.

Krishna nudged him. Raghu took a long look at the crowd and began:

'Today, I am not going to give any speech; instead I'm going to share my experience. Earlier I used to study a lot